SNAPSHOTS FROM THE PAST

When young widow Helen meets Ed her future at last seems bright. Her newfound happiness seems complete until a terrifying new shadow falls across her life. Someone is watching her, tracking her movements and sending her chilling photographs through the post — pictures relating to her past. Soon Helen can trust no one, and when her suspicions finally fall on Ed, their relationship is shattered. But who is Helen's tormentor? And will she and Ed ever get together again?

ANGELA DRAKE

SNAPSHOTS FROM THE PAST

Complete and Unabridged

LINFORD
Leicester

First published in Great Britain in 2006

First Linford Edition
published 2007

British Library CIP Data

Drake, Angela
  Snapshots from the past.—Large print ed.—
Linford romance library
  1. Love stories
  2. Large type books
  I. Title
  823.9'14 [F]

  ISBN 978–1–84617–905–1

Published by
F. A. Thorpe (Publishing)
Anstey, Leicestershire

Set by Words & Graphics Ltd.
Anstey, Leicestershire
Printed and bound in Great Britain by
T. J. International Ltd., Padstow, Cornwall

This book is printed on acid-free paper

1

It was five years since Helen had been in Prague. On her last visit she had been with her husband, Peter, and wildly in love. She had felt blessed, as though she were the luckiest woman in the world. Then three summers later he had been killed in a tragic accident. And now she was once again in the Czech capital to receive an award on Peter's behalf, and she was entirely alone.

Looking out of her hotel window across the roof tops of the old town, Helen recalled the shock and grief following Peter's death. She had been left desolate and crippled with loneliness, her days dark and purposeless. It was only through the kindness of friends and her parents that she gradually began to rebuild her life.

She had no enthusiasm for returning

to her former work as a fashion journalist and there was no real need to be employed as Peter had left her well provided for with substantial life insurance. There was also the proceeds from his bestselling autobiography about the joys and perils of being a top British athlete. But as she was not yet thirty she had not wanted to live the life of a wealthy, idle widow and so she had taken a training course in design and couture, then set up a small business making wedding and ball gowns for private clients.

She turned from the window, wondering if it had been a mistake to come back to the city where she had experienced such dizzy happiness with Peter. What if she wasn't up to dealing with the triggering of old memories? Stop it, she told herself. Of course you can handle it. And who else should receive this tribute to Peter's sporting achievements except his former wife?

She pulled off her in-flight clothes, took a shower then slipped into pink linen jeans and a crisp white shirt. Stepping from the lift into the marble and gilt foyer of the hotel she saw that delegates for the international sports conference were arriving in a steady stream, dragging huge cases through the entry doors.

At the far end of the foyer she could see into the palatial banqueting room where the award ceremony was to be held that evening. Rows of white-clothed tables glittered with cutlery and glasses. She went to look at the programme of events board at the far end of the foyer, noting the times of the reception, the dinner and then the presentation of awards.

A man came to stand beside her, studying the board with interest. After a few moments he turned to Helen. 'Hello,' he said simply. His smile was open and direct, yet not at all flirtatious.

'Hello,' Helen said back. There was something about the man's face and his manner which caught her attention. He was tall and broad-shouldered, dressed in crumpled blue jeans and a dark green T-shirt casual to the point of shabby. But his hazel eyes had a steady and watchful quality which she found unusual and appealing.

'Are you one of this group?' he asked, gesturing to the information board. 'A top sportswoman? Or just a hanger-on like me?'

'Neither. I'm the widow of a former top sprinter.' She saw a quick flash from light to dark in his eyes, a fleeting unspoken message of sympathy at her loss. 'And you?' she asked. 'What sort of hanging-on do you do?'

He laughed. 'I'm a lawyer. I specialise in accident and injury compensation related to sporting activities. I suppose that's why I get invited along to these occasions — they never know when they might need me.' As he spoke his eyes seemed to be lit from within, vivid and glinting with life.

She noticed the interest in his glance, his appraisal of her face and figure. And she was glad that she had changed out of her crumpled travel clothes and that she'd made the effort to have her shoulder-length black hair cut and styled before she left England. How strange to be feeling like this, she thought. Disconcerting and at the same time enlivening.

A voice sounded behind them. 'Ed! There you are!' A small blonde woman with elfin features and a shaggy haircut came to stand up close to him. Beside him she was like a little terrier looking up at a shaggy brown bear. A very admiring and seductive terrier. 'I need a word,' she said, winningly.

'Nice to meet you,' Helen told the man, smiling and walking away, having no wish to play gooseberry. But even so, she was aware of his voice echoing in her head, a deep furry growl of a voice, threaded with warmth and humour.

She made her way to the nearest entry to the Mustek underground system and joined the little throng waiting for the train. Side by side with the camcorder-carrying tourists were young Pravian men and women with sharp haircuts and stylish clothes.

At the Old Town stop she got off and made her way to the ancient Town Hall Clock, noting that it was almost time for it to strike the hour. A small crowd of people were gathering to watch the procession of mechanical figures which would move around the clock's face as it chimed.

She recalled standing in this very spot with Peter, hanging on to his arm and looking up at him, in much the same way the small blonde woman in the hotel had looked at the man beside the programme board. As the tinkling metallic chimes rang out, she felt an ache of loneliness and longing.

And then suddenly there was shock and a stab of pain as her bag was wrenched from her shoulder. She turned, spotting a youth making a swift exit through the crowd. Furious and determined she sprinted after him. She was a fast mover, having kept up the running sessions she used to go on with Peter. In seconds she was gaining on him. He turned into a narrow alleyway.

'Hey, I want my bag back,' she shouted. The thief turned. He was pale and skinny and she could see the fear and desperation in his eyes. Without warning he came heading straight for her, cannoning against her, thumping her so hard in the stomach that the air seemed to be driven out of her lungs. She stumbled and fell on to the stone cobbles with a dull thud.

Dazed with shock she lay on the ground for a few moments, her heart racing with alarm. A young Pravian woman stopped and helped her up. 'Are you all right?' she asked in perfect English. 'Do you need a doctor? I can call on my mobile?'

'No, no. I'm fine, thank you,' Helen said. 'Please don't worry. I'm not hurt.'

The woman smiled. 'Take care, then.'

Helen made her way back to the Old Town Square. Her legs felt decidedly wobbly and tiny furred dots of light kept floating in front of her eyes. When she reached the medieval St Nicholas church with its crown-like cupolas she sank down on to the broad steps which led up to the great door, and dipped her head between her knees.

The dots of light began to fade and she became hopeful that she was not going to fall into a faint like a distressed Victorian heroine. She felt a hand on the small of her back.

'Are you OK? Can you sit up?'

She knew immediately who was speaking, that low growl was unmistakable.

She looked up into his face. 'I'm minus my handbag and a bit bruised, but I think I'm going to live.' Despite her little show of irony, she could still feel her heart thundering with outrage and alarm. Putting a hand up to her cheekbone, she touched the tender spot where the fall on the cobbles had grazed her.

'You've been attacked?'

'I got targeted by a bag-snatcher,' she

explained. 'I legged it after him, which turned out to be a bad idea. He body-butted me and I ended up flat on the cobbles.'

'Dear, oh, dear.'

'I don't think it was personal,' she said with a rueful grin. 'He just wanted my bag.'

'Do you want me to go with you to the police to report what's happened?'

'No. I haven't lost anything important. Just my Prague guide book and some loose change. Let him have it, maybe he needs it more than I do.'

'That's a pretty generous way of looking at things,' he said. 'Hey! You're still shaking!'

'I'm all right,' she insisted.

'You need a cup of good strong coffee, laced with brandy,' he said. 'I know just the place.' He took her arm and placed it through his. 'Come on.'

'Are you always this bossy?' she asked, aiming for a light tone.

'Oh, I like to see what I can get away with.' He pressed her arm more

9

securely against his.

Helen suddenly found tears in her eyes, grateful that he had chosen to take care of her, rather than walk away and leave her to her usual stubborn self-reliance.

He took her to a dimly-lit basement café-bar accessed by a flight of ancient steps with deep, foot-shaped grooves in their centres. Seating her on a worn velvet banquette in an empty corner, he ordered coffee, brandy and sweet pastries.

'I've a vague idea this bar is one of those the city executioners used to gather in for a jar after a hard day's work,' he said, settling himself by her side. 'Around four hundred years ago.'

'Well, that's certainly something to cheer me up.' She pulled a wry face as he smiled across at her. She felt a hum of connection between them, and she knew he could sense it. 'My name's Helen,' she said. 'Helen Lashley.'

'I'm Ed Connelly.' He was still smiling.

The waitress brought their order. The first sip of coffee was hugely welcome. 'I'm trying to place your accent,' Helen told him. 'But I can't make up my mind. Not quite Irish, not quite Scottish.'

'Right on target!' he congratulated her. 'I was born and raised in Dublin, then moved to Glasgow when I was twelve. A bit of a mongrel. Where are you from, Helen?'

'I was born and brought up in a little village in Surrey. And now I live in London.'

'A rose from the garden of England,' he quipped.

She smiled and took a sip of her brandy. It slid down her throat and sent a glow through her.

'Are you on your own sight-seeing in Prague?' he asked.

'I'm here to receive an award in commemoration of my late husband's sporting achievements. Peter Lashley.' She paused. 'You'll probably remember him.'

Ed thought for a few moments. 'Sure, I do. He was a fine athlete. You must feel very proud.' He hesitated. 'I seem to remember he was killed in a road accident, is that right?'

'Yes.' She looked down into her coffee cup. Memories swirled and shifted. 'He liked speed of all kinds, not just running. He went out one evening for a spin on his motorbike — and he never came back.'

'I'm so sorry,' Ed said quietly. She could feel his sympathy, solid and genuine.

'Are you married, Ed?' she asked, rather surprising herself. It wasn't normally her style to ask a relative stranger such a personal question.

'I'm a single parent. I have a daughter aged seven,' he said.

It seemed an unusual, incomplete response, but his gaze was frank and level. 'Do you have children, Helen?' he asked gently.

'No.' She paused for a moment. 'Peter and I planned to have a family, but we never got around to it. We were both involved in our careers. He was training most of the time and I was making my way as an assistant fashion editor with a national magazine. We thought there was plenty of time before we settled down to have children.' She looked down at her coffee, a wave of sadness washing through her.

Ed placed his hand over hers, stroking her skin with gentle fingers. She felt quite at ease with him and made no attempt to brush away the teardrop which slid down her cheek. His touch was warm and reassuring.

Later that evening in the banqueting room, smiling and composed in an ankle-length sheath dress of cream silk, she stepped forward to accept the silver goblet engraved with Peter's name and a list of his sporting achievements.

Placing her sheet of notes on the lectern she glanced at the rows of interested faces and began to read in a low, steady voice, describing the stages of Peter's career and the endless hours of training he had undergone in order to achieve his numerous successes.

She held herself firmly back from straying into emotional territory, banishing any glimpses of the wonderful closeness with Peter which had been so brutally stripped away.

As she drew the speech to a close there was a warm burst of applause and she sat down feeling satisfied and relieved. Looking along the tables she noticed Ed, sitting with the elfin-faced woman. As her eyes caught his, he smiled, raising his glass, and she felt her heart give a tiny lurch.

She straightened her spine. Don't even think about it, she told herself.

The next morning, as she breakfasted in the hotel's dining-room, Ed came up to her table. 'Good morning,' he said, cheerily. 'How are the bruises?'

'Beginning to go through the colours of the rainbow, as bruises do,' she told him.

He smiled. 'Are you flying home today?'

'Four o'clock flight.'

'Then maybe you've time to come for a little trip with me? That's if you'd like to.'

She hesitated. She felt unaccountably pleased to see him, and somehow that sounded a warning. 'Why not?' she responded on impulse, amazed to hear the light-hearted flirtation in her voice.

Half-an-hour later she was sitting next to him on a tram making its way to the outskirts of the city. After they got off, he led her up a steep cobbled path which ended in a delightful sloping garden, at the end of which nestled a low white-painted villa.

'It's called Bertramka,' he told her. 'It used to belong to friends of Mozart and provided a hidey-hole for him whenever he stayed in Prague.'

'Are you a Mozart enthusiast?' she teased, as he paid their fee and they walked over polished wood floors in search of musical history.

'Just an admirer,' he said, gesturing her to look at the walls which were

15

covered with original handwritten fragments of Mozart's music framed in stern black wood. Further on there were letters the composer had written to his father and wife whilst on his travels. Pages and pages of them.

'He wrote all this himself,' Helen exclaimed. 'Without a computer. No wonder he died young.'

Ed laughed. 'He was a great communicator. It's a good job he didn't have the use of a mobile phone, he'd have run up huge bills.'

Helen felt herself relax. She had wondered if this mystery trip would be a mistake. But she was truly enjoying his company, feeling quite at ease.

As she turned to smile at him he put out his hand, running a finger over the bruise on her cheekbone. 'How are you?' he said softly. 'Really?'

'I'm fine,' Helen said. She could sense a connection shimmering between them like a live current. The attraction she had felt the day before had been far more than a flash in the pan.

Ed steered her in companionable silence through the final display rooms then walked with her into the garden. They made their way up a sloping lawn which led to a small wood. He sat down on a wooden bench under a horse chestnut tree and she placed herself beside him. Fat conkers dropped from the trees with rhythmic thumps.

'I'd like to tell you a bit about myself,' he said. 'And my daughter, Maisie.' Suddenly his jokey manner had vanished. 'I want to be completely honest with you, Helen. For the simple reason that I'd very much like to get to know you better.' He paused. 'And I want you to know something of my rather unusual family circumstances.'

Helen noted the intensity in his voice and her curiosity about his family situation intensified.

'You see,' he began, 'as far as Maisie is concerned, she has no mother. She just has me, we're a genuine one parent family. Maisie was the outcome of a fling I had with a local girl I met on a holiday in Italy.' He paused. 'Are you shocked by that?'

'No,' she told him quietly.

'This girl contacted me some months later and told me she was pregnant, and that I was the father. She also told me that she needed money from me. No way must her fiancé find out about the affair.'

Helen stared at him. 'But, Ed, how did you know the baby was yours?'

'I didn't. But I believed her. And I wanted her to marry me.'

Helen was alarmed to find herself feeling a tiny stab of jealousy at the thought of Ed's passionate fling and his determination to marry this unknown girl.

'I wanted my child, you see. I wanted to hold it in my arms. To live it. To bring it up.'

Helen heard the strength of feeling in his words. 'But, presumably, you didn't persuade her to marry you.'

'Quite right. She preferred the Italian fiancé. I believe he came from an old

18

Venetian family, with the appropriate trappings of money and a palazzo on the Grand Canal. Anyway, I told her I'd support her for the few months in London before the child was born and pay any medical expenses involved. And afterwards I'd keep silent forever, providing she let me adopt the baby and never tried to contact either of us.'

'You really did want that baby,' Helen murmured, realising how single-minded and self-willed he must have been to make it all happen.

'Yes, I did want that baby,' he said. 'And I got Maisie. And she's a miracle.'

There was a long pause. Helen thought about what he had told her, and understood how important Maisie was to him, and how great a responsibility he felt towards his child.

'What happened to Maisie's mother?' she asked.

'She went back to Venice and married her fiancé.' He picked up a conker from the grass and lobbed it into the wood.

19

'She wouldn't even hold Maisie after the birth. She just wanted to forget the whole episode. End of story.'

Helen looked at him in amazement. 'It's a very remarkable one.'

Ed reached out and took her hands in his. She turned to him. The firm line of his jaw and the depth of feeling in his eyes stopped her heart.

'You see, Helen,' he said quietly, 'if I get involved with anyone, then automatically Maisie does too. And I've promised myself that I'll never knowingly do anything to hurt her or make her unhappy.'

It took some time for the words to sink in, and then to read between the lines. I'm on trial, Helen thought. He's vetting me as a possible mother figure for his little girl, because if he gets involved with me, then it follows that I get involved with Maisie.

'I think I can guess what you're driving at Ed,' she said, aiming to keep her voice calm and reasonable. 'You're thinking that maybe I'm not a good bet to join your single-parent family. You're thinking that a lonely young widow with a tragic past might not to be the sort of woman likely to provide a stable mother figure for your daughter.' Horrified at what she had said, and the bitterness in her tone, she tore her hands from his and sprang up.

He sat watching, his expression gentle and reflective. 'Helen — I didn't mean that. And I didn't mean to offend you. I'm sorry.'

'There's no need,' she said formally. 'I understand.' Disappointment hollowed her insides. She didn't know quite what to do next and Ed seemed disinclined to help her.

She felt hurt, and a sense of terrible injustice seized her. 'Oh, let's just forget it, Ed,' she exclaimed, swinging away from him and striding purposefully across the lawn to the little cobbled lane. Perversely she wanted him to come after her. But he didn't.

When she reached the main road she had the luck to spot and wave down a taxi. Within twenty minutes she was back at the hotel, collecting her things and checking out. Two hours later she was on a British Airways flight to Heathrow.

2

Helen forbade herself any brooding after the events in Prague, although a picture of Ed had slotted itself firmly into her memory, and she felt growing regret about the abrupt way in which she had brought their brief friendship to a close. She gradually settled back into her routine of work and socialising with friends. The summer faded. A chill came into the air and the trees turned from flame to gold.

Her current bride-to-be client, for whom she was creating a cunningly fitted 1960s style sheath dress, was causing her some problems. On her third fitting the client was a twelve pounds lighter than the last time Helen had seen her. The dress would require major reconstruction work.

'Are you planning to get any thinner?' Helen asked, as she crawled around her client, pinning extra darts into the gown's waistline.

'Oh, I don't know. Maybe. Everyone slims down for their wedding day, don't they?' The bride-to-be beamed with satisfaction as she plucked at the heavy duchesse satin, pulling it away from her waistline into peaks to demonstrate how much spare there was.

Helen resisted the temptation to stick a pin in her.

'I bet you don't have to worry about your weight,' the client told Helen. 'You're as thin as a greyhound.'

'I wasn't always like this,' Helen said, through a mouthful of pins. 'In fact a few years ago I was carrying quite a few more pounds than now.'

'Which diet did you use? I'm on the banana and cucumber one.'

'I didn't diet. It just . . . happened.' Shock can do that, she thought. And misery.

'Lucky you!'

'If only you knew,' Helen murmured under her breath.

After the client had left, Helen tacked the newly-cut seams by hand, then swathed the dress in tissue and laid it on one side. Going through to her bedroom she changed from her working gear into tailored trousers and a jacket, then ran out to her car and set off to her parents' house.

It was her mother's birthday and she was planning to take her out for lunch. She allowed herself plenty of time, knowing from past experience that driving from her flat in west London to rural Surrey could take as long as two hours.

Her parents lived in an old-fashioned village which had an ancient stone church and an old windmill whose sails still worked. Their house was detached and substantial, set in a large, ornate garden.

Helen drew her car to a halt in the semi-circular drive and reached for the big bunch of lilies and the *Miss Dior* fragrance she had brought as presents.

She let herself in through the back door which led into a large kitchen with wooden beams and an old green Aga which was breathing out heat. It was the room which had been the haven of her childhood. She recalled walking in from school and letting the comforting warmth and the smell of baking steal around her. And her mother, Annette, had always been there to greet her, smiling in welcome.

But today the room was empty. It looked as though her mother was somewhere around as the long varnished table where she created illustrations for children's books was strewn with pencil sketches and water colour paintings in varying stages of development.

Her paint brushes were standing in the little bottles of water she used to clean them. A paint-spattered rag was crumpled into a ball as though suddenly thrown down and left.

Helen walked through into the inner hallway. 'Hello, there! It's me, Helen! Anybody home?'

All was still and silent. A shiver of apprehension ran through her. When her cellphone rang inside her bag she gave a start of alarm.

Her father's voice came on the line, brisk and to the point. 'Helen, I'm sorry — I've got bad news.'

Helen braced herself. If her father said it was bad news, he wasn't joking.

'Your mother's had a fall in the woods, whilst she was out with the dog. One of her dog-walking friends found her and called for an ambulance. She's been taken to the local hospital.'

'Poor Mum! Do you know what injuries she's got?'

'They tell me she's waiting for X-rays. It seems she might have cracked a bone.'

'Oh dear. I'll go along and see her right away.'

'I'd appreciate that,' her father said, in his formal way. 'I'm at a meeting in Amsterdam, but I'm taking a flight home as soon as I can get away. Can you hold the fort until I get back?' The words came out like shots from a gun.

'Of course.'

'Apparently they think there might be complications, they'll probably need to admit her. I'm always telling her not to go clambering about in the woods,' her father said wearily, 'but she won't listen.'

'What about Archie?' Helen asked. 'Mum'll be more worried about him than anything else.'

'Ah, yes,' he said with a resigned sigh. 'He's been taken to the local police station.'

'Don't worry, Dad, I'll go and pick him up and keep him happy.'

'Good. Yes. Look, Helen, I've got to . . .'

'I know, work calls. I'll take care of everything, it's no problem.'

Clicking off the connection she ran upstairs to her mother's room and packed nightwear, sponge bag and slippers into a holdall. Dropping the luggage into the boot of her soft-top MGF she roared off to the local police station to collect Archie, her mother's adored pet.

On seeing Helen he leapt forward with joy and almost knocked her to the ground. He was a leggy, hairy mongrel with the strength of Goliath and a heart of gold. Helen had no option but to let him sit on the front passenger seat as there simply wasn't room for him anywhere else. 'Keep still, and lie down,' she told him. The tone of her voice made him look at her with new assessment. He lowered himself carefully on to the seat, curled into a compact ball and went to sleep.

At the hospital she found her mother sitting propped against a mound of pillows, making a determined effort to look cheerful. Her face was bruised and grazed and her hair lay in matted clumps on the pillow. Her left leg was in plaster from the knee down.

She winced in pain as Helen wrapped her arms around her. 'I'm all right,' she said fiercely.

'I should hope so,' Helen said sternly,

29

kissing her cheek. 'What were you doing to take a fall? Climbing around on one of those out-of-the-way paths fit only for goats?'

Annette gave a guilty smile.

'Oh, Mum. You and your dog-walking exploits. And on your birthday, too.'

'I know. I should be old enough to know better.'

'So, what's the damage?'

'Oh, just a few cuts and bruises. And a splintered ankle bone.'

Helen shook her head in affectionate despair.

'What I'm really worrying about is Archie,' Annette said. 'The ambulance people said he'd been taken to the police station — '

Helen broke in. 'I've already picked him up. I knew you'd be desperate if you thought he wasn't getting his usual five-star hotel treatment. I'll take him home with me for a day or two if you like.'

'Oh, bless you, Helen. You know

Dad's not much use with dogs.'

Helen smiled. Her parents were one of the happiest long-married couples she knew. But quite different from each other in temperament and interests. Whilst Annette was artistic and sentimental about children and animals, her father was deeply absorbed in the running of his accountancy firm and hopelessly undomesticated.

As Helen prepared to leave, Annette reached out and caught her hand. 'I'm sorry to cause you this worry, Helen. You of all people don't need it.' Unspoken between them were the memories of the days following Peter's sudden death and Helen's long battle to haul herself out of the pit of grief and despair.

'It was an accident, there's no need to apologise. Just you take things easy and take care of yourself,' Helen said softly. 'No falling out of bed and breaking the other ankle. You're much too precious for that.'

It was around seven when she arrived

31

back at her flat. As she drew the car to a halt in the road outside, she noticed two figures standing at the door. For a split second her body tensed with alarm. And then she registered a tall, well-made man with a young girl, and her nerves fizzed with quite a different emotion.

She could see the girl's face in the light from the street lamp. A strong and beautiful face, strangely adult, the winged cheekbones those of a warrior queen. But something around the mouth was unmistakably her father's.

'Hello!' Ed greeted her with his warm, direct smile. 'Maisie and I were on our way for a Chinese. We wondered if you'd like to join us.'

Archie had given one or two guard-doggy growls on spotting strange people threatening Helen's territory. Once he realised they were her friends he began to wag his tail. Maisie went up to him and held out her hand. Instantly he sat, gazing at her with irresistible appeal. She knelt on the step and put her arms around him. Within seconds they were friends for life. Helen could swear Archie was smiling.

'Well, well!' Ed said in dry tones.

Maisie was crooning to Archie now, telling him what a super dog he was. She turned and looked at her father with huge appeal in her big dark eyes.

'I'm getting the feeling we won't be able to separate these two for a while,' Ed commented.

'I think a takeaway might be in order,' Helen said, her mind racing with silent speculation as to why Ed had suddenly appeared out of the blue. And at the same time feeling delight and anticipation stealing through her like a warming sip of brandy. 'Crispy duck and fried seaweed for me. And I think Archie's rather partial to egg fried rice.'

Ed grinned and went away, leaving Helen to unlock her front door and persuade Maisie and Archie to continue their new love affair indoors.

Maisie sat cross-legged on the kitchen floor, gently massaging Archie's ears whilst

Helen started setting the table. 'I've got a pet mouse,' she told Helen. 'He's very nice, but not like a dog. Is Archie a Labradog?'

'He's a kind of mixture dog. Part greyhound, part collie. He belongs to my mum, but I'm looking after him for a few days.'

'He's a one-off,' Maisie said, with satisfaction. She looked around her. 'Is this your house?'

'Just the downstairs part.'

'Are you a lawyer, like my daddy?'

'No. I'm a dressmaker.'

'Have you got any children?'

'No.'

'My mummy lives in Italy,' Maisie said with cheery matter-of-factness. 'But I've never seen her.'

Helen judged there was a good deal of food for thought in those few simple words. She thought about parentage and blood connections. About the preciousness of love between children and parents, and the pain of separation. She glanced down at Maisie who was continuing to stroke Archie, her hands gentle yet assured.

Helen looked for signs of wistfulness in her face, unspoken questions about the mysterious mother she had never seen. But her expression revealed no conflict or regret. She seemed perfectly happy and serene to be talking with Helen and fondling her new canine friend.

Helen recalled having read somewhere that children were usually secure and content as long as they had one stable, loving parent to share their life and guide them into adulthood. She found herself hoping very much that would be the case for Ed's disarming daughter.

Maisie looked up again. 'Are you going to be Daddy's girlfriend?'

Helen smiled. 'I'm Daddy's friend,' she said simply.

Maisie gave her a quick, critical appraisal, making Helen girlishly self-conscious of anything which a child's shrewd eyes might disapprove of. She put up a hand to her hair, which had arranged itself into a riot of wild curls through the day as the autumn mist had settled on it.

Maisie gave her a big smile and Helen smiled back, sensing the child's approval and willingness to be friends. She, in turn had really taken to Ed's little girl, warming to her energy, her piercing curiosity and her childish candour. Her hair was light brown like her father's, but her eyes were a deep contrasting hyacinth blue. She was wearing flared denim jeans and a pink T-shirt decorated with a blue appliqué butterfly. Perfect.

Helen decided to try a little childlike frankness herself. 'Does Daddy have many girlfriends?' she asked, setting out glasses beside each mat on the table.

'No.' Maisie gave Archie some more kisses. 'He and Tamsin were friends when I was five or six. And now I'm seven. Can I see the dresses you make?'

Helen led the way into her workroom

and switched on the lights.

Maisie was instantly drawn to the tailors' dummy which had once belonged to Helen's grandmother.

'You can alter her shape,' Helen explained, squeezing the centre of the dummy to make its waist more slender. 'I call her Maud. I'm not quite sure why.'

Maisie ran her hands over the headless, limbless figure. 'Hello, Maud. You're lovely.'

Helen picked up the dress she was making for the bride who kept getting thinner and slipped it over the dummy's head. 'I've made Maud the same shape as the lady who's going to wear this dress. So as I'm going along I can keep trying it on Maud to see if it fits, even when the lady's not here.'

'That's cool,' Maisie said, going on to examine Helen's fat pin cushion, her huge cutting shears and the boxes of buttons and scraps of material left over from all the dresses she had made.

'It's like Aladdin's cave,' Maisie

decided. Once again she looked up at Helen, her eyes full of interested appraisal.

'If you'd like any buttons or scraps of material to take home, just help yourself,' Helen told her.

Maisie sifted through the buttons and put a few on one side. 'Could you make something for me, Helen?'

Helen smiled. 'Yes, of course. What would you like?'

'I'd like a Calamity Jane cowgirl outfit.' She gazed at Helen, her eyes wide with hope and appeal.

'You mean like Doris Day wears in the film?' Already Helen's mind was humming, thinking of possible fabrics, making sketches, designing a pattern.

'Mmm. Daddy and I have looked in the shops but we can't find one.'

'Have you got a DVD of the film?'

Maisie nodded vigorously. 'It's my very most favourite.'

'Well, if I can watch it I might be able to work out what kind of materials we'll need. And then — I could make a start.'

Maisie let out a breath of happiness and they grinned at each other, their excitement at the project fizzing between them.

Ed returned with the food and a bottle of wine. Helen laid the cartons on the table and they all sat down to eat. From time to time Ed caught Helen's eye and smiled at her. An adult, conspiratorial smile that made her heart give little leaps.

'This is nice,' Maisie said, as she forked up noodles. 'Daddy sometimes cooks spaghetti Bolognese, but he can't cook Chinese.'

'I'll have to try harder,' Ed murmured with a wry smile.

'What's your favourite food, Maisie?' Helen asked.

'Fried eggs. Daddy does super fried eggs.' Maisie threw her father a look filled with transparent affection and pride.

Helen observed the two of them with growing pleasure, impressed by the bond of closeness and the easy affection between father and daughter.

When they had finished supper Maisie helped Helen to clear the table and then announced her need for the bathroom. Archie trotted after her like Mary's little lamb and sat outside the bathroom door, on guard.

As Helen stood at the sink filling the kettle, Ed got up and slid his arms around her. She leaned back against him.

His fingers stroked her collar bone. 'I hope we can spend some time together.'

Helen was uncertain for a while, part of her longing to be with him, part of her fearful of laying herself open to all the dangers of falling in love again. She took his hands and pulled his arms around her waist.

'What will Maisie think about this?'

'I think she'll be fine. Although I don't know how she's going to feel now there's this love affair with the dog.'

'You must promise her she can come and see Archie whenever she likes.' Helen turned around in his arms. 'Why did you come now, Ed?' she asked curiously. 'And how did you find me?'

'It took some time,' he admitted. 'There are quite a few Lashleys in the London directory. I just kept going through them, ringing until eventually I got your answerphone.'

'That was very persistent of you.' She smiled. 'I'm impressed.'

The next morning, when she met him for breakfast, she knew that any plans for caution about getting involved with Ed were futile. And the wonderful thing was, she didn't care.

After breakfast they took Archie for a long walk in the park. Ed held her hand and dropped occasional feathery kisses on her cheek.

'Maisie is a lovely child,' she told Ed. 'You must be very proud of her. And I can see how precious she is to you.' She was trying to tell him how much she had taken to Maisie, and how she now understood what he had been driving at when they had talked in the garden of the Villa Bertramka in

Prague. 'She's the love of your life,' Helen finished softly.

He was silent for a few moments. 'Maybe. But only for a time. You're just living on borrowed time with your child's love. They grow up and then they fall in love and then they want to belong to someone else. And that's how it should be.' He pulled her closer against him. 'A man needs a mate, Helen.'

When they got back to the flat it was time for him to set off to collect Maisie. As the moment came to say goodbye Helen found herself wanting to cling to him in case he should vanish forever into thin air. He gave her a long, loving kiss as they stood by the open door of his car.

Helen held her breath, bracing herself for those doom-laden words, *I'll call you.* She realised how insecure she still was. But then her husband, Peter, had simply walked out of her life and never come back. She supposed she could forgive herself for being anxious.

'Tomorrow,' Ed said. 'My place. Any time after eleven-thirty. Lunch, tea, dinner. Whatever you want.'

She stood watching and waving as his car disappeared into Kensington High Street, then ran up the steps to her front door, joy and optimism zinging inside her. She picked up the morning post and sorted through the letters.

There was a postcard from her friend, Katya, who was in Egypt and a letter of appreciation from a client for whom she had made an Edwardian-style wedding gown. The last and biggest envelope was brown and business-like. Helen slit it open expecting some advertising material or a circular. Inside there were simply two photographs with no accompanying message.

Helen frowned as the realisation of what she was looking at hit her — snapshots of herself. One was a head and shoulders shot showing her contemplating a display in a shop window. She couldn't make out the shop, or

43

what it was which had caught her attention in the window, but it was a recent picture judging by her hairstyle and had most probably been taken in Oxford Street. Yet it had been taken without her knowledge and by no-one she could think of.

The second picture was more perplexing as she couldn't immediately put a date on it. It showed a Helen decidedly younger than she was now, but the background gave no clue as to where it had been taken, or when.

Helen stared at the image with growing bewilderment. It was a shot of which she had no recollection whatsoever. She looked at the envelope. The name and address were neatly typed, and the postmark *London W1*, which was of little help.

Giving a little sigh of irritation she pushed the photographs back into the envelope and threw them into a drawer where she kept odds and ends which she couldn't quite bring herself to throw away. I've got an unknown admirer she told herself, refusing to waste time worrying about odd and unexpected mail. All she wanted to do was let her mind travel blissfully over the last magical hours with Ed.

3

Ed folded Helen into his and Maisie's life. She began to spend a good deal of time at his house in Earls Court; a red-brick Victorian villa with white plaster cherubs over the front door.

She was also spending time with her mother who had now been discharged from hospital, although she needed the aid of two sticks in order to walk. There was concern because the fracture in her ankle bone was reluctant to heal, and her confidence in her mobility seemed damaged. There was no question of her being able to exercise Archie and so Helen adopted him on an open-ended basis, much to Maisie's joy.

Helen found Ed a wonderful companion. He was generous, funny, teasing and loving, and one of the least moody people she had ever met. She loved his lit-up smile, the way he hummed with energy and curiosity about everything he did, the way he listened with close attention to her most trivial remarks. He included her in the family Sunday lunch at his parents' crumbling old rectory in Kent where she received a warm welcome.

He made her a part of his group of lawyer friends, whisking her off to impromptu suppers, drawing her into the full swing of life once again. Helen was interested to be reintroduced to the elfin-faced blonde she had seen him with in Prague. Her name was Liza, and she was one of the lawyers on his team.

She had a handsome and devoted boyfriend who made it very clear that Liza was his property. So that's all right Helen thought with a wry internal smile, recalling her previous spark of jealousy regarding the effervescent Liza.

Ed was also keen to draw her into his passion for music. They went to concerts at the Albert Hall, and to the opera at Covent Garden. Whilst she enjoyed the concerts she found the world of opera somewhat daunting. One evening, after an hour and a half of what seemed to Helen like endless screeching, she stood next to him in the bar at the interval, sipping a glass of mineral water and looking thoughtful.

'You're not enjoying this, are you?' Ed enquired, ever observant.

'No, sorry!' She gave an ironic smile. 'But for you, Ed, I'll put up with it.'

He placed a kiss on the tip of her nose. 'And for you, my darling, I'll forego it.' He took her hand and led her away into the teeming streets around the opera house where they found a dark wine bar and sat together, savouring a glass of burgundy and drinking in each other's company.

Meanwhile she and Maisie were getting to know each other as they put their heads together to plan the creation of a *Calamity Jane* outfit. They went to the nearby library and took out a huge glossy picture book filled with vivid stills from the great movies of the 50s and 60s.

From this Helen was able to make an authentic sketch of Doris Day's cowgirl suit, from which she would eventually design and cut a paper pattern.

'Can you really make a cowgirl outfit?' Maisie asked, as she watched Helen shading in her drawing of the fringed top and cowgirl trousers which would form the basis of the costume.

'Really and truly,' Helen said, giving her a swift hug. 'But it might take quite a few weeks.'

'It must be very difficult.'

'Not when you know how to do it,' Helen explained. 'I went to college to learn and I've had lots of practice making things for my clients.'

'Can I learn to sew?' Maisie's face shone with eagerness. 'Will you show me how?'

'Of course I will. And then you'll be able to help me, if you want to.'

Maisie gave a sigh of happiness. 'Cool!'

⋆ ⋆ ⋆

Ed sat in his office in west London, checking a report his secretary had word-processed for him. It concerned a woman who was claiming compensation following the crushing of her hand when a car rammed her against a wall.

In addition to losing the use of two of her fingers the accident had caused considerable emotional damage. As an injury lawyer, Ed had a good deal of experience of people suffering emotional fragmentation long after their physical symptoms had been dealt with. He signed the report and moved from his desk to stand by the window, looking down into the busy road below.

His thoughts turned to Helen, as they did so often since the two of them had got together. He understood that Helen had a many-sided personality and that, like all people who have suffered the tragic sudden loss of a loved one, she was probably still emotionally fragile.

It was her fierce self reliance combined with her vulnerability which had instantly drawn him to her from the very first moment of their meeting. He had been fascinated by the way her wide-open grey eyes had concentrated on his face when they talked together. She was not conventionally pretty, her facial bones were too strong, the curves almost razor-sharp. But for Ed she was beautiful, and tantalisingly mysterious.

When he had first kissed her he had been instinctively gentle and tender, sensing that she needed the kind of kiss you would give a child in trouble. Her lips had been warm, yet tentative, and when he finally drew back he knew that something momentous had happened to him. There was no going back.

His delight in being with her outweighed everything. And he knew that Maisie was enchanted with her, for Helen had that instinctive honesty and sympathy which make a child feel totally secure. She would make a wonderful mother.

He went back to his desk and tidied the papers strewn over it into a neat pile. He had never been this much in love before. It was fantastic. And just a touch scary.

★ ★ ★

Helen let herself into her flat and went straight into her studio to switch on the lights and check that the heating was on at full. In a few minutes her bride-to-be client was coming to pick up her dress. Helen had finished it a couple of days before. It was hanging beside her sewing table, loosely swathed in yards of protective tissue paper. She was pleased with the finished result, happy with the clear carved lines of the dress and its dignified simplicity.

Her client arrived promptly and chewed her lips with anxious anticipation as Helen slowly pulled the tissue away from the dress and revealed it in its svelte, sculpted glory.

The client stared at it for a few moments, then clasped her hands in delight. 'Oh, it's beautiful. It's a work of art. I hardly dare try it on.'

Helen smiled, warmed by the young woman's enthusiasm. When the seemingly endless row of tiny hooks and eyes were fastened, the bride turned to face the full-length mirror. One glance at her told Helen that all the hard work had been worthwhile. The heavy satin curved itself around the client's figure and transformed her into a beauty. She looked gorgeous.

'Now I can't bear to take it off!' she protested.

Together she and Helen tucked the dress into its bed of tissue, then eased it into a huge zip-up bag embossed with Helen's name.

'Thank you, thank you!' the bride called out as she made her way to the front door, holding the dress bag as tenderly as though it were a new-born baby.

Helen closed the door behind her, smiling with satisfaction. She picked up the mail which had just arrived and sorted swiftly through the envelopes.

When she came to a brown one bearing a *London W1* postmark, her heart gave a lurch of unease. She ripped the top from the envelope, steeled herself, and then pulled out the contents.

There were two more photographs. The first showed Helen in her car with Archie sitting in the passenger seat. It was impossible to make out where it had been taken; the background was out of focus and just a blur. But it had clearly been taken within the last few weeks. Archie had never travelled in her current car before that.

Beneath it was a picture of Helen from much earlier days. Once again it was a picture she could neither place, nor recall. She guessed it had been taken around ten years before when she was approaching twenty.

She stared at the picture, prickles of sensation snaking over her skull. What was the sender trying to tell her? And why?

It was a Saturday afternoon and Helen and Maisie had spent an hour or so in central London searching out some suitable fabric for the *Calamity Jane* outfit. But so far they hadn't found anything suitable.

'We could try the charity shops,' Helen suggested.

'But they just have clothes that are already made,' Maisie pointed out.

'Yes. But ready-made clothes can always be unpicked and made into something else.'

Maisie looked up at her and grinned. 'Ooh, it sounds like magic!'

After rifling through the clothes in three different shops with no success, Helen was on the point of suggesting they should go home and try another day, when she heard a little squeak from Maisie. She had found a 1960s ginger-coloured suede coat which had fallen off its hanger and lay screwed up in a heap on the floor.

Maisie picked it up and began to brush off the fluff and dust. She looked at Helen, her eyes shining. 'Will this do?'

'Simply perfect,' Helen told her, getting out her purse as they made their way to the sales counter.

On the tube going back home, Maisie was in a fever of excitement and couldn't wait to show Ed the battered, soiled treasure she and Helen had discovered.

'I think you've got your work cut out there,' Ed remarked dryly to Helen, eyeing the ancient coat doubtfully.

'Trust me.' Helen reached up on tiptoe and kissed him.

★ ★ ★

Helen's mother had returned to her illustration work. The kitchen table was strewn with the cheering clutter of her water colours and the rainbow-hued jars of water she dipped her brushes into. Her two sticks were balanced on either side of her chair. She struggled to her feet as Helen came into the room.

'You didn't need to get up,' Helen chided her, kissing her cheek.

56

'Oh, I'm so tired of sitting still or tottering about like a ninety-year-old. I've got to try and get fully mobile again.'

'You will. Give it time,' Helen reassured her. 'It's good to see you working again.'

Annette smiled down at her work in progress. 'This is a commission I couldn't resist. A book jacket for a marvellous new young novelist.'

Helen looked over her shoulder at the painting. The picture of a mischievous-looking white pony prancing in a bright green field drew the eye like a magnet.

'I'd be over the moon if I were the author,' Helen commented.

'Thanks for that, darling,' Annette said, loading her brush with more colour. 'I was worried I might have lost my touch. I'm afraid this accident has really set me back. Every time I stand up, or make a sudden movement I feel so wobbly.'

'Oh, Mum! Poor you. But you will get better, you just need to give it time.'

'I know. You're right.' She made a gesture of dismissal with her hands. 'Anyway that's enough about me. How's your new man?'

'He's fine.' Helen's face softened into a dreamy smile. 'He's lovely. And funny. And kind.'

'And will we be meeting him some day?' Annette enquired, with a quizzical smile.

Helen made a grimace of apology. 'I'll fix up a meeting for us all. Soon, I promise.'

'There's no pressure from Dad and me, Helen. You know that.'

Helen nodded. 'I keep thinking about the past,' she told her mother. 'About Peter and how happy we were . . . ' Her voice died away.

Annette reached out and placed her hand over Helen's. 'What happened with Peter is so very unlikely to happen again.'

'Yes — I know.' Helen sighed. Once again she recalled that fateful afternoon when Peter had roared off on his bike to a training session and been tragically mown down by a speeding car.

Except he hadn't gone to a training session. He'd gone to visit a married woman with whom he'd been having a year long secret affair. The accident had happened just outside her house. She had been the one who found him. The one who contacted the emergency services and then telephoned Helen. The one who had been Helen's best friend since primary school.

Despite her shock and grief it had not taken Helen long to work out what must have been going on, and when she had eventually forced herself to go through Peter's clothes and correspondence weeks later, she had found plenty of damning corroboration. The hurt and humiliation had been terrible. And more bitter still it had had to be endured in the spotlight of Peter's former fame.

The newspapers couldn't get enough angles on the young widow who had been betrayed by her best friend. The story ran for weeks.

But Ed would never betray me, she kept telling herself. She believed in him. He was her new love. He would be the love of her life. And yet a tiny voice still sounded a warning. She had begun to wonder if when you've been hurt very badly, you ever heal.

'A new relationship is a big step,' her mother said. 'And, you know even as a child you were never one to wear your heart on your sleeve. And I don't suppose you've changed.'

Helen smiled. 'You're right. But I've known Ed for three months now. I think it's time I let my heart have a little more freedom!' She looked out of the window, watching the trees wave their bare branches against the sky. Her thoughts turned yet again to the troubling, unsolicited photographs. She took in a breath. 'Talking of my childhood, Mum, have you still got the old family photographs Dad took years ago?'

'Yes, I think we have. They're mostly

still in their packets. I keep thinking I'll get around to going through them and making an album.'

'I'll do it,' Helen said. 'I'd like to.'

'Good.' Annette gave a wry smile. 'Why not let Ed help? It might be a good way of breaking the ice before you take the plunge of letting him meet us in person! And talking of meeting him, maybe you, him and Maisie will all come for lunch on Sunday. I'll leave it with you.'

When Helen left her parents' house later on, she had with her a bag full of photographs and a sense of sudden urgency to reach the privacy of her flat and look through them without delay. She cleared a space on her sewing table and started to take the photographs from their packets.

Although the various shots were not individually labelled, the packets were all clearly dated, enabling her to arrange the pictures in chronological order. She laid them out in neat rows, deliberately avoiding any detailed examination of them.

When the task was finished she went to the kitchen and made herself strong black coffee.

As she poured boiling water over the grounds she found her eyes sliding towards the most recently arrived envelope. She had not yet been able to bring herself to open it. This whole issue of being sent anonymous mail was beginning to get to her.

Maybe she should refuse to collude in the cruel game the sender was playing. Maybe she should refuse to open any new mail, simply tear up the envelopes and their contents and burn them.

Impatient with that line of reasoning, she set her coffee cup down and tore open the envelope. There was just one picture. It showed a gawky-legged ten or eleven-year-old Helen lying on her stomach in the garden of her Surrey home, reading a book. Her legs were bent up and lazily crossed. Her attention was deeply focused on her book. It was a photograph which seemed to capture an intensely private moment in a young girl's life. One which should only have been taken by family or close friends.

But when Helen walked through into her studio she found that there was no corresponding picture amongst the snapshots her father had taken. Moreover the shot had been taken in black and white, whilst her father consistently used colour.

The obvious conclusion was that someone other than her father had taken the picture. A thrill of disquiet went through her as she got to grips with the inevitable conclusion that some unknown person had been photographing her over the years without anyone else's knowledge.

The puzzle of what the sender was trying to tell her seemed harder and harder to fathom. As did their motive in contacting her. But more worrying than both of those questions, was the issue of what they were planning to do next.

4

Ed was in the house on his own when she let herself in. Maisie had been invited to a friend's house for supper and was sleeping over. He was sitting in his study, working on his computer. Sometimes he brought reports home to work on when he was especially busy. He didn't hear her come into the room as he was listening to a CD of a Mozart opera, playing at full volume.

Helen tiptoed silently towards him and placed a soft kiss on the back of his neck. 'What are you up to?' she asked, nuzzling him and inhaling the smell of his skin.

'No good, of course.' As she peered over his shoulder he swiftly closed the file he was working on. He hated anyone to read his reports before he had honed them to perfection. 'For my eyes only,' he smiled.

'But we're in love,' she murmured. 'We shouldn't have any secrets from each other.'

He pulled her head down to kiss. 'Being in love is probably a very good reason for keeping at least one or two secrets,' he teased.

Helen glanced at his raised eyebrows. Was he letting her know that he was well aware of her tendency to keep certain feelings and anxieties locked away in her own thoughts?

Well, since the issue of secrets had come up, she thought that surely now was the time to share one of them with him. At least the one that was dancing in the very front row of her thoughts.

'Ed,' she began, then was forced to break off as the piercing soprano on the CD suddenly burst into fortissimo shrieks making it impossible to hold a conversation. Ed smiled and held up his hand, clearly wanting to give his full attention to this little gem of passionate Mozart.

She withdrew her arm from his neck

and padded off to the kitchen, feeling a touch rejected. There was a bottle of Sancerre chilling in the fridge. She filled two large glasses, then looked in the cupboard for crisps or nuts. She had hardly eaten all day and her stomach felt hollow. There was just a jar of black olives, which she shook into a dish.

Tip-toeing back to Ed's desk, she placed the glass beside his laptop and stroked a finger along the back of his neck. 'Relax. Take a break.'

'Mmm, I could be tempted,' he murmured, folding down the lid of the computer and putting it to sleep.

Helen took two large sips of wine and felt an instantly calming effect.

'I've booked for us to go away at the weekend,' he said suddenly. 'Paris. The Eiffel Tower, Disneyland, dark little bistros. You, me and Maisie.'

Helen was caught out by the unexpectedness of his generous offer. 'Oh!'

'Is there a problem?' Ed enquired.

'Well, I'd hoped we might go and visit my parents on Sunday,' she said lamely, wondering why she was being so defensive and churlish. There was no definite arrangement with her parents, and Ed's planning a surprise weekend in France was sweet of him. But then in recent years she no longer welcomed surprises.

'Dear, dear,' he said mildly. He turned to look at her. 'I shouldn't have taken it for granted. That you'd be free and not have any other plans.'

'Oh, Ed!' she exclaimed. 'Of course you should have taken it for granted.' She took some more long sips of wine.

He was watching her. She had a sense of being an unpredictable animal he had taken into his house to take care of, and that she was snapping at the hand that was feeding her.

'It's all right, Helen,' he said quietly. 'You have your own life, and I respect that.' He turned away, making no attempt to persuade her, and she knew that she had hurt him. She now longed

67

for the clock to be turned back and for him to repeat his invitation to Paris. She also wanted quite desperately to confide in him about the photographs — but the moment seemed to have passed, fleeting and fragile.

She sat down on the sofa and drank more wine. Ed came and sat beside her, his shoulder touching hers. The music had gone quiet. Maybe that fragile moment was retrievable after all. 'Ed — '

The speakers suddenly exploded with sound. It sounded as though someone was being thrown into hell. Her nerves shrieked. She leapt up as though she had been shot, made for the CD player and jabbed at the off button. 'For goodness sake, can't we have a bit of peace?'

The resulting silence was awful. She swallowed painfully, not knowing where to look or what to do next. Avoiding Ed's glance she stumbled out of the room and went to the cloakroom in the hallway.

Her head was swimming with the effects of the wine and, staring in the mirror, she saw that her hair was a mass of untamed curls and that her eyes were wild and glittery.

She splashed cold water on her cheeks, then moulded her hair into some sort of submission. Smoothing her blue wool sweater she went slowly back to Ed's study where he was sitting exactly where she had left him.

His eyes connected with hers and he got up and came towards her. She laid her burning face against his shoulder. 'Ed, I'm so, so sorry.'

'No worries.' His tone was light and forgiving but the words were not as reassuring as she would have wished. He rubbed his hand up and down her spine.

She stood there, shocked and numb. She hated what she had done. She knew he didn't deserve it.

★ ★ ★

In the end Helen was saved from making a decision about going to Paris when her mother fell down the stairs and broke her arm. Her father's voice over the phone sounded tinged with panic and she realised that immediate help and support was required.

But she still made time to drive Ed and Maisie to the airport where Ed gave her a quizzical farewell smile before kissing her gently.

'I'm sorry your mummy's poorly,' Maisie told Helen, hugging her tight. 'But I wish you were coming with us.'

Helen put her hands around the little girl's face. 'Have a lovely time. And whilst you're away, I'll make sure to do some more sewing on *Calamity Jane*. That's a promise.'

She watched them disappear through the doors to the concourse, then drove straight to her parents' house, her mind full of her growing love for Ed and Maisie. She made a resolution that when he got back from this short break she would stop hugging her secrets to herself and confide in him fully.

Her father greeted her, his face heavy with anxiety. 'Your mum's asleep at the moment. Her wrist bone's in plaster. The doctors tell me her ankle bone is healing better than they hoped, but I'm not so sure. She still seems afraid of putting any weight on it.'

He was sitting at the kitchen table. There was a half-eaten bowl of cereal in front of him and a puddle of milk on the table top. He had a day's growth of silver stubble on his cheeks and he suddenly looked old and diminished, not at all the sharp-edged professional Helen had always known.

'I'm taking two weeks' leave from work, and I'm thinking of taking retirement,' he said abruptly.

'Dad! Are you serious?' Helen was astonished. She had always thought he would work until he dropped.

'Your mother's going to need a lot of help. I'm her husband, and I'm the one who should do it. We're neither of us getting any younger you know,' he concluded regretfully.

Helen laid her hand on his and squeezed it in sympathy.

'I've neglected her,' he said sadly. 'I've always taken her for granted. And now she's injured and incapacitated I realise just how much she means to me — and how selfish I've been.'

'Dad, you've worked hard for years and provided a wonderful home and lifestyle for me and Mum. That wasn't selfishness.'

'Yes, it was,' he said regretfully. 'I've always loved my work and that was what I wanted to do, even when we'd got enough money for me to slow down. Your mother would have liked to go travelling, but I never had the time and she didn't want to go on her own.'

'No-one gets things right all the time,' Helen told him. 'And you've been a great husband and a lovely dad — even if you weren't always around.'

She got up and started preparing fresh coffee and tidying the kitchen which was beginning to have an air of neglect. Her father accepted the coffee with a wan smile. 'Thank goodness you're around to help us out, Helen. We'd be in a mess without you.'

Helen spent the next two days in quiet domesticity; shopping, making meals, doing the laundry, walking Archie and ensuring that neither of her parents were sitting around moping. And all the time she found her thoughts winging across the sea to Ed and Maisie, wondering what they were doing, wishing she was with them, longing for them to return home.

A few hours before they were due to land at Gatwick she returned to the flat to pick up some clothes and check her mail. She held her breath as she sorted through the envelopes. But there was no unwelcome brown envelope to deal with and she found herself laughing out loud with relief.

Having glanced into all the rooms to make sure all was well, she ran out to her car, her mood light and positive as she looked forward to seeing Ed and

Maisie once again.

There was a folded sheet of white paper tucked beneath one of the windscreen wipers. She pulled it open, expecting an advertising leaflet. There was just a simple, handwritten message. *I love you, darling*.

Helen clutched at her stomach, suddenly feeling very sick.

'Helen, Helen!' Maisie chanted as she and Ed stepped out of the taxi that had brought them from the airport.

Helen held out her arms and Maisie hurled herself into them. Behind them Ed stood looking on, one eyebrow raised, a smile curving his mouth. Helen felt her heart swell, her nerves tinged with electric excitement. 'I've missed you so much,' she murmured as he slid his arm around her.

Helen cooked spaghetti Bolognese with plenty of garlic and herbs because it was Maisie's favourite. 'This is fantastic,' she told Helen, forking up the strands and in between talking excitedly about her brief holiday.

'A lady came to our table when we were having supper at the hotel,' she told Helen in confiding tones.

'And why was that?'

'She wanted us to go to her table and have supper with her. Daddy said she could come and sit at ours if she liked.'

'And did she?'

'Yes. We didn't really want her. I didn't like her. She said I'd be quite safe in bed at the hotel and then she and Daddy could go out for a drink.'

Helen was intrigued by this picture of Ed being chatted up by a predatory woman. She supposed she shouldn't be surprised, he was a very attractive man. 'So what happened then?'

'Oh, Daddy said I was allowed to stay up late on holidays.' Maisie shrugged, losing interest now the story had reached its climax.

After supper she followed Helen about, happily nuzzling against her, and insisting on three bedtime stories. Eventually Helen settled her under the duvet and gently stroked her hair.

Ed was in his den sipping whisky and water. Soft piano music drifted from the stereo speakers. As Helen sat beside him, he took her hand and pressed his lips against the palm. 'How was your weekend?' he asked, his voice low and tender. 'How are your parents?'

He listened carefully as she gave him a short résumé.

'I shouldn't have sprung Paris on you as a surprise,' he told her. 'I'm sorry. And, having thought about it, I don't think I'd be too pleased if anyone did that to me.'

'I'm sorry too,' she murmured. 'That I've been on edge and touchy.'

There was a pause. 'Ed, there's something I need to tell you.'

'This sounds ominous,' he said lightly.

'I hope it isn't. But it's something that's been on my mind.' As slowly and as calmly as possible she told him about the anonymously-sent photographs, and how they did not match any of the pictures in the family album. And about

76

the worrying message left on her car.

Ed listened with total attention. A flicker of emotion passed over his face as she finished speaking. 'Why have you kept this to yourself, Helen?' he asked eventually, and there was something in his voice she had never heard before which sent prickles of dismay through her nerves. 'When I was here for you?'

'I suppose I wanted to pretend it wasn't important,' she said, realising how feeble that sounded.

He got up and went to stand by the window, looking out into the orange glow that was London's darkness. She watched him, her disquiet escalating.

'Ed, I don't know why I didn't tell you,' she protested. 'If it's any consolation, I haven't told anyone else.'

'I'm not anyone else,' he pointed out coldly.

Helen closed her eyes, feeling raw and vulnerable in the face of his quiet hostility. She hadn't a clue how to make things better, and she certainly didn't want to dig herself in deeper. A feeling of desolation and helplessness swept over her.

'So what happens now?' he asked with icy politeness. 'Do you want me to help you with this?'

'Of course. What do you think we should do?' she asked, snatching at the opportunity to be given another chance.

'I'm not sure. Not until I've seen these photographs for myself. Are you going to let me see them?'

'I'll go to the flat and get them now.'

He made a dismissive gesture with his hand. 'No, I'm not happy with that. I don't want you to go back to the flat alone.'

'I'll be all right.'

He grasped her wrist with uncharacteristic urgency. 'Helen, this is serious. You could have been in danger all these weeks. Helen!'

'I know,' she admitted miserably.

'OK, then. Just tell me where this stuff is. I'll go and get it right now. You look after Maisie.'

She told him where to look, her nerves jangling with distress as he strode out of the door. He was back in forty-five minutes, grim-faced as he tossed the envelope on to his desktop.

'You open it,' Helen said, cringing as he pulled out the contents and spread them on the desk.

She sat down on the sofa. It was as though Ed had taken charge and she'd passed the problem on to him. She didn't think she could bear to go through the anonymous sender's collection ever again.

'You said that none of these photographs are from your personal family album.' He sounded like a prosecution lawyer grilling the defendant.

'That's right.'

'Which suggests some unknown person has taken them?'

'Yes.'

'Some unknown person who has been tracking you and taking pictures of you over the years?'

'Yes.'

'And who knows the current car you drive and where you live?'

'Yes.' Her voice had sunk to a whisper. 'But I have absolutely no idea who it could be.'

'Dear, oh dear.' His voice was calm, but she could tell how appalled he was. He turned back to the pictures. 'Whoever's sending these doesn't seem to know much about using a camera,' he observed reflectively. 'The focus and the lighting are pretty haphazard. It seems that all they're interested in is getting pictures of you.'

She knew his mind would be feverishly humming with speculation and theories. Would he spot something she had missed?

'What do you think the message means?' she asked him shakily.

'Well, either someone's developed an obsession with you or they're just playing a cruel joke.'

'Maybe the message has nothing to do with the photographs. Maybe it wasn't meant for me, someone just got the wrong car,' she suggested, clutching at straws.

He swung around to look at her. 'Do you really believe that?'

'No.'

He was silent for a time. 'What can be the motive for doing all this?' he mused. 'There are no demands, no direct threats.'

'Well at least that's something,' she said, aiming for a positive tone.

'I'm not so sure. Who is to say this couldn't all turn into something very unpleasant?'

'Do you think I should go to the police?' she asked.

'Most probably, yes. But then, I doubt what they could do, apart from mounting a surveillance on your house and car, which I don't think they'd consider an option, given the costs.'

'What would you do, Ed, if you were on the receiving end of this?' she demanded.

He paused. 'I'd have a good long look into my past. Lovers, antagonists,

81

clients who were unstable or might harbour a grudge. You name it.'

She was silent for a few moments. 'I never had any lovers except Peter,' she said. 'I had the usual fallouts with friends in my teens, but nothing serious. I'm aware of some people in my past who I didn't get on with so well, but no way would I regard them as enemies.'

As she spoke the word *enemies* her mind suddenly threw up a connection from the past, and a pulse ran through her nerves. No, surely not. She pushed the hateful thought to one side.

'Fair enough.' He fell silent once more. 'Helen, I'm finding it hard to understand why you've kept all this secret from me.' His voice was calm, but she heard the underlying note of accusation.

'I wanted to pretend it was nothing,' she pleaded. 'I thought if I ignored it, it would go away.'

'Given that your life has become closely connected with Maisie's and mine, I'm surprised it didn't occur to you that she and I could be in danger too.'

Helen stared at his grim, set face. He was telling her that she had put Maisie at risk. And he had a point. Waves of guilt and humiliation washed over her. 'I'm sorry,' she mumbled.

She could see that he was icily furious with her, and she felt that she deserved it.

'I'm going to bed,' he said abruptly. He gestured to the anonymous mail on the desk. 'Could you put all that somewhere where Maisie has no chance of stumbling over it? And I'd be grateful if you'd take it back to your flat as soon as possible.'

He turned at the door. 'Good night, Helen.'

She sat very still, shocked and inwardly shaking as though he had thrown an exploding bomb at her and it had only narrowly missed. After a time she got up, pushed the hateful mail back into its envelope and pushed them to the bottom of her handbag.

Sleep was impossible that night whilst her mind went over and over their bitter discussion. Eventually she slipped out of her bed and rummaged in her bag for the sleeping pills she had kept on hand for those nights when the grief about Peter suddenly struck again. She hadn't needed them for weeks. She shook one out of the bottle and swallowed it. Ten minutes later she sank down into a deep, black sleep.

5

It was past nine when she wakened. She washed her face in cold water then trailed miserably down to the kitchen and switched on the kettle.

Her mobile began to trill. Please let it be Ed. She looked around frantically, having no idea where she had last left it. It went on singing to itself in some secret place as she made a frantic search. Eventually she located it in the pocket of her coat which was flung over a chair in the hall. 'Hello!'

'Helen, it's Dad here.' Disappointment flooded through her, and then a spark of alarm. 'I'm phoning from the hospital. Your mum got up in the night and then collapsed on the bathroom floor. I had to call the ambulance. She's undergoing tests, but so far they can't say what's wrong.' The words came out in a wooden recital of disaster. He sounded terrible; weary and desperately worried.

Helen's heart sank. 'I'll come right away.'

When he didn't argue, she knew things were serious.

The new anxiety made her pull herself together. She drank a cup of strong coffee and ate an apple. Peering out of the window she saw there had been a heavy frost in the night. She went upstairs and pulled on black jeans and a dark green sweater.

She found her father sitting in the corridor adjacent to the Accident and Emergency Department. He glanced up when she touched his shoulder. His eyes looked blank as though the lights inside them had been turned off. He nodded a brief acknowledgment of her presence. 'Hello, dear.'

She sat down beside him. 'Dad, she'll be OK. She's always been very strong and healthy.' She tried to believe her own reassuring words.

'I thought I was going to lose her,' he

said. 'She was dizzy and sweating. And then she said she was going to lie down on the floor, because if she didn't she'd just fall down. And after that she just passed out. I thought she was having a stroke.'

Helen felt a spark of blind panic. She looked at her father, sitting like a marble figure, silent and wretched, and knew she had to be strong for him. She took his hand in hers and held it firmly, rubbing her thumb over the skin as though he were a scared child.

In time a young house doctor came to tell them he could not yet give them a definite diagnosis regarding Annette's condition. 'She's dizzy and nauseous when she tries to move,' he explained. 'But she's conscious now, and quite lucid.'

'That must be good news,' Helen said, schooling her voice not to tremble.

'Has she had a stroke?' her father asked the doctor abruptly.

'No.'

'A heart attack?'

'No. There are no clinical signs of either.'

'So what is it?'

The doctor gave an apologetic smile. 'I'm sorry, we just can't say. It could be some kind of virus infection. We've taken blood samples, but we won't know the results of all of them for a day or two.'

Helen's father groaned, his tension unbearable.

The doctor looked at Helen. 'I suggest you go and get something to eat and in an hour or so she'll probably feel able to see you both.'

Her father gave a weary sigh. Helen took hold of him and steered him towards the café in the lobby. 'I don't want anything to eat,' he said.

'OK. Shall we go for a walkabout?'

He shrugged. Helen guided him through the main doors. As they walked through the small garden area, her mobile rang, making her nerves jangle. 'Yes!'

'Helen?'

'Ed!' She closed her eyes in frustration. 'Look, I'm sorry — '

'Is this a bad time to talk?' he asked.

'You could say so.' She gave him a swift verbal sketch of the situation.

'What can I do to help?' His voice was filled with warmth and concern.

Oh Ed! She wanted to throw restraint to the winds and offer him a passionate apology for her secrecy and lack of trust, and an even more passionate affirmation of how much she loved him. But her father was there beside her, his face grey with fear and agitation. 'I don't really know just at the moment. But thanks for asking.' She injected as much love as she could into the matter-of-fact words.

'I'm here at the end of the phone if you need me. I'll collect Maisie from school this afternoon.'

'No, no. I'll be able — '

'I'll do it. I'll see you very soon.'

She clicked off the connection. It was as though new life had been breathed into her. The sharp emotions of the night before had been smoothed away by Ed's simple kindness and understanding.

'I'm taking you to a very nice café around the corner for an early lunch,' she told her father. 'No arguments. You need it.'

Having persuaded him to eat two scrambled eggs on toast, Helen took his arm and walked him back to the hospital where they found Annette lying prone in bed looking dazed and exhausted by her ordeal.

'Oh, my dear!' her father said, gazing down at her with distress.

'You mustn't worry, Clive,' she told him. 'I'll be all right. Just give me time.'

'Have they found out what's wrong yet?' Helen's father demanded.

She shook her head. 'If I get to be any more of a nuisance to you both, you must promise to have me put down like a tired old dog,' she said, her tone a mixture of joking and despair. Her eyelids drooped as though she couldn't hold them up.

'I'm going to get to the bottom of this,' Helen's father said, jumping up and nobbling the harassed doctor they had seen earlier and demanding a diagnosis.

Helen listened as the doctor soothed her father with promises that they were not holding anything back, that as soon as they had any positive information they would give him it.

In the end he gave in and came back to sit beside Annette. 'My poor darling,' he kept murmuring as he sat holding his sleeping wife's hand, oblivious of the hours passing.

Eventually Helen managed to prise him away from his vigil and drove him home. It was dropping dusk as they went down the drive towards the dark and empty house and she had a rush of anxiety on her father's behalf, wondering how he would cope on his own, weighed down with worry about her mother.

'Shall I come in with you?' she asked. 'Will you be OK?'

'It's this not knowing what's the matter with her that's getting to me,' he said, letting out a long sigh. 'But I'm quite able to look after myself, if that's what is worrying you, Helen.'

Helen held her hands up in surrender, assuring him she had no wish to play the over-anxious daughter. For the first time that day he gave a dry smile and she felt a warm spark of closeness with him. She kissed him on the cheek as they parted.

As she drove away the reassuring words she had offered her father sounded in her ears like hollow clichés, and the concern about her mother gnawed at her insides like a physical pain.

✱　✱　✱

Maisie was watching her DVD of *Calamity Jane* when Helen arrived back at Earls Court. Doris Day was clambering around the outside of a hurtling stagecoach belting out the promise that when she got home she was fixing to stay.

'Whip crack away,' Maisie belted back. Helen bent down and dropped a kiss on the top of her head. Archie gambolled up and rested his head on Maisie's delicate knees, gazing at her with beseeching brown eyes that could melt the railings in Regent's Park.

Helen was interested to see who would win the battle for attention — Doris or Archie. She didn't find out. Ed came stealing up behind her, sweeping the hair away from the back of her neck and pressing a kiss on the skin beneath. His arms slid around her. He held her very close and it felt wonderful.

She wanted it to go on for ever, being so near to him, so safe from all the worries of the outside world. 'Sorry about last night,' he murmured into her ear.

He went out to get a takeaway Chinese meal. Maisie set the table, then she and Archie cuddled up together on the rug and continued with *Calamity Jane* who was taking a long time to get her troubles resolved as Maisie kept stopping the disc and replaying her favourite parts of the action.

After supper, when Maisie had gone upstairs to bed, Ed and Helen went into his study to relax. They had just settled down when the door bell sounded.

'I'll get it,' Ed said, making his way to the front door.

Helen heard him open the door and then the low murmur of voices. When he reappeared his colleague, Liza, was with him. She was clutching a bottle of wine and wearing an exaggeratedly apologetic expression.

'Hi there, Helen. I'm so sorry to burst in like this. But I need Ed's advice, and I just couldn't wait a moment longer before I spoke to him.' She threw him one of her winsome smiles.

'She tells me she's been head-hunted by another firm,' Ed explained. 'Which is good news for her, but not so good for us.'

'Oh, don't flatter me,' Liza protested, slanting him a whimsical glance.

'You'll be hard to replace,' he told her.

Liza curled herself delicately on the sofa. With her slender legs in tight stretchy jeans and her fluffy pink sweater she looked like an exotic pedigree kitten. 'The problem is, I'm in a complete agony of indecision. I don't know whether to go or to stay where I am.' She turned to Helen. 'You see, I'm really very happy working at Ed's place,' she explained.

'Are they offering to stuff your tiny fists with gold?' Ed enquired, with a twinkling grin.

'Absolutely. Frighteningly tempting amounts.'

'So, are you wanting me to match their offer?'

Liza gave a rueful shrug. 'Money, money, money!' she exclaimed, with a dramatic sigh. 'It's always the bottom line.'

'This sounds serious,' Helen said

with an understanding smile. 'I'll leave you two in peace to talk business.'

Ignoring Liza's sweet protests about chasing her away, she got up and went to check that Maisie was happy and settled.

She saw Ed the next morning when she called round.

'I have a client to see in Brighton,' he said. 'I'm going to get the seven-thirty train. Can you take Maisie to school?'

Helen sat up and pushed the hair from her drowsy face. 'Yes, of course.'

He held her face between his hands. 'Is everything all right?' he asked. 'I'm sorry we didn't get to talk yesterday evening.'

She knew he was referring to his coldness two nights before when she had shared her worries about the unwanted photographs. 'Yes,' she reassured him. 'And I can understand why you were upset.'

'Well, don't forget, I'm always here for you. And you can trust me, even with the nastiest secrets.'

'I know.' She reached up and touched his lips with her fingertips. 'I do love you,' she whispered.

In the kitchen she put a pan of water to heat on the stove in preparation for boiling Maisie's breakfast egg. Then she phoned the hospital and was told that her mother had had a comfortable night. But there was still no clear diagnosis of her condition.

She went back upstairs and gently shook Maisie's shoulder. Archie woke first and nipped smartly off the bed, shaking himself vigorously.

'You wicked dog,' Helen told him affectionately.

'It was my fault,' said Maisie, snapping up instantly from fathomless sleep into full life. 'I told him he could get on.' The twinkle of irresistible appeal in her eyes was exactly like that of her father.

After Maisie had eaten her egg and toast soldiers they walked along to school, taking Archie with them. Maisie skipped and danced along the streets, energy and well-being crackling in the air around her.

'What do you want for Christmas, Helen?' she asked. Christmas! She'd hardly given it a thought. The decorations had been up in the London streets for so long, she hardly noticed them. 'I'll have to think about it,' she said. 'What do you want?'

'For my *Calamity Jane* outfit to be ready. Please.'

'Of course it will be. But I'd like to get you something else, as well.'

'I'll have a think,' she said. 'Just like you will be doing.' She smiled up at Helen, reminding her how good life was since she became a part of Ed and Maisie's family.

Maisie reached up for a kiss when they got to the school gates, and Helen hugged her tight for a few seconds, then watched her blend into the moving throng of children in the playground.

She had planned to go to her flat that morning to be on hand to field any queries for new commissions. And, of course, to check the post, to see if there was any message from her photograph-obsessed pursuer. Any clue to his identity.

What she really wanted to do was go back to Ed's place, just to be there.

Telling herself she would be back well in time to collect Maisie and provide a welcoming snack for her before preparing supper, she got into her car and edged through the traffic to Kensington. As she was parking the car outside her flat she noticed a woman standing on the steps beside the front door.

She turned as Helen ran up behind her. She was around Helen's mother's age, tall and angular, her face lined and ravaged by time, yet still beautiful, her silver hair loose and wavy around her shoulders.

Helen introduced herself. 'Can I help you?'

The woman looked at her, her face slowly lighting up with a warm smile. 'My name's Eleanor Holt. I've come about a wedding dress,' she said.

Helen unlocked the door and ushered

99

her through, scooping up the post and swiftly ascertaining there was nothing which demanded her instant attention. No suspicious large brown envelope — thank goodness.

'A friend of mine recommended you,' the woman said. 'She told me you were very good.'

Helen smiled. 'Well, what can I do to prove it to you?'

Eleanor Holt sat down, crossing long slender legs. She unbuttoned her elegant navy wool coat, revealing a simple cream dress beneath. 'I need to tell you a little about myself,' she said with a slightly hesitant smile. 'I'm fifty-nine, and I'm getting married for the first time ever. So I'm wanting the dress of a lifetime. Literally.'

Helen smiled in acknowledgement of this unusual story. She made it a rule never to make comments on her clients' personal revelations, although she always aimed to appear sympathetic.

Her main task was to create a

fabulous garment. And already she was finding inspiration from Eleanor Holt's appearance and demeanour to begin creating the gown just for her.

Soon they were in discussion about the ins and outs of silver or turquoise velvet as against gold brocade. Helen showed Eleanor some swatches of fabric, then opened her sketch pad and made a quick pencil drawing, a medieval style gown with long flowing lines and an elegant train fanning out from the hips.

Eleanor looked delighted. And by the time she left an hour later, slipping a card giving her mobile phone number on the hall table, Helen found herself with an intriguing new commission and the exhilarating sense of confidence and purpose which always came with the prospect of an interesting new work project.

She spent an hour or so looking through her book of period fashions, developing the sketch and experimentally draping some gold satin around Maud.

By lunchtime she began to feel hungry and padded to the kitchen, switching on the kettle and peering into the biscuit tin. Wondering if her father had left any messages about her mother's progress she dug her phone from her bag and activated voicemail.

There was just one call, timed just after nine earlier in the morning.

'*Hi, Ed,*' a bright voice gushed. '*It's me, Liza. Listen, I'm really sorry, but I couldn't make it for the seven-thirty. I'll get the eight-thirty and see you at the hotel as soon as possible. Take care now.*'

Helen dropped the phone back into her bag as though it had stung her. It was Ed's phone, he must have forgotten it, and she had picked it up by mistake.

Liquid rushed into her mouth, borne on a wave of nausea. Suspicion and hateful jealousy clutched at her stomach and her heart began to beat in thick lumpy bursts.

Stop it! She told herself. Stop it! You love Ed, you know he would never betray you, never do anything to hurt you. It's a perfectly harmless message. They're going to see a client together. That's all there is to it.

She paced around the room like a caged animal. But why meet at a hotel?

She went back to her workroom and began making a new sketch. But the enthusiasm with which she had worked earlier had all drained away. The more she tried to grasp it, the faster it disappeared. She laid down her pencil, her thoughts tracking back to the phone call.

She thought of listening to it again, then forbade herself. But the suspicion within was spreading like spilt liquid, poisoning her emotions, stripping away her rational common sense.

Once again she recalled going through dead Peter's clothes, could taste again the bitterness of betrayal as she found all the proof she needed. She stood in the hallway, her arms wrapped tightly around herself. But Ed was different. She trusted him, completely.

She thought about their meeting in Prague, the instant connection between them. The way he had been there to take care of her after her bag was snatched. The understanding and love which had grown between them.

Suddenly her brain began to form connections it had never made before. How was it that Ed had been so conveniently on hand in the Old Town Square in Prague to help her following her mugging? Had he been following her? Had he been stalking her? He had chided her for keeping secrets, but maybe he had some of his own. Had he known her in the past without her being aware? Could he be the person who was sending the photographs. 'No! No!' she moaned, out loud.

But the questions went on buzzing in her head like naughty children who would not be silenced.

'Stop it!' she hissed at them.

She had to go back to the house in Earls Court. She had to disprove all her shameful misgivings.

It was now early afternoon. She had planned to visit her mother in hospital and then go on to collect Maisie. But she realised there wasn't time, she would run the risk of getting stuck in the traffic and not being on time at the school. She rang the hospital and asked them to tell her mother she'd be there to see her in the evening.

She judged Ed wouldn't be back until early evening at the soonest. As she drove back to his house she calculated that she would have an hour to search before it was time to set off to meet Maisie.

The coolness and clarity of her resolution shocked her. As she opened the front door and felt the emptiness and hush within she could hear the drumming of her heart.

'Hello!' she called out, testing the silence. 'I'm home.'

She walked through the downstairs rooms. 'Ed! I'm back.' She went slowly up the stairs, calling all the time. There was just stillness and quiet.

She started in his study, taking the little key he kept buried in the box of paper clips on the desktop and unlocking the drawers. She found nothing incriminating. No notes or love letters.

She rifled through the stacks of CDs. She ran her fingers over the spines of the books he kept on his shelves. Nothing.

Slowly she went upstairs, into his bedroom. Why are you doing this, Helen?

She opened his wardrobe and reached out to touch his shirts and jackets. As her fingers connected with the fabrics a tiny shivering thrill darted through her nerves.

She dipped her fingers in the pockets like the stereotype of the suspicious wife, searching for tell-tale handker-chiefs with lipstick stains on them. But she discovered nothing.

She noticed a brown leather storage box at the back of the wardrobe. Tentatively she reached out to place her fingers around it, and just at the moment there was the sudden blare of a car horn outside in the road, loud and insistent.

Instinctively she retracted her hand as though she were a thief reacting to the sound of a burglar alarm. The sound of the horn went on, and kept going.

She went to the window and saw that the car parked next to hers had its alarm lights winking. The noise from the horn was jarring and intrusive. She just hoped the owner of the car would come and restore the peace.

She went back to the wardrobe, took out the box and placed it on the carpet. Lifting the lid she saw that it contained some neat stashes of paper.

Her ears were ringing now with the noise from the car horn, jangling through her nerves. She lifted the nearest wodge of papers from the box. It was loosely tied with maroon satin ribbon. Ed had written on the front in his stylish Italic script: *Maisie — August 1988*.

She swallowed. The sense of trespass burning inside her. What she had stumbled on was so private, so intensely intimate between Ed and Maisie and the woman who had given birth to her and given her up. She put them on one side and took out another bundle of papers. They were birth and death certificates, mostly quite old and relating to Ed's family.

She closed her eyes, overwhelmed with a rush of horror at what she was doing. The car horn blared on, reverberating in her ears like some doom laden warning.

When she opened her eyes again Ed was standing in the doorway looking at her. She stared back at him transfixed. His face was uncharacteristically both motionless and unreadable. But his eyes were like guns. 'What are you doing Helen?' he asked quietly.

Her backbone sagged. She couldn't speak.

He came to stand beside her as she knelt by the bed, her body flooding with shame. She watched his hand move in front of her as he reached down for the papers she had just examined.

'You were welcome to any of this information. You only had to ask,' he said.

Her throat was full and swollen. There was nothing she could say without incriminating herself. 'Yes,' she said eventually.

'So, did you find what you were looking for?' he queried, getting down to the essentials of the matter.

She shook her head, dumb with misery.

He looked down at her as she knelt at his feet. 'Oh, Helen. When did you lose your capacity for trust?'

She got up. It was still impossible to speak. She looked him in the eye, telling him from her soul how sorry she was. She didn't expect to be forgiven, she certainly didn't deserve it, but hope still flickered. He had amazed her before.

He was utterly still, utterly silent. Just looking at her, seeing all the bad things there inside her. Mistrust and betrayal.

'I'll go,' she said. 'I'll get out of your life.'

He stood aside as she walked past him. He made no move to stop her. Her hip brushed against his arm, but there was no spark of contact. Even with that brief touch she could feel his hostility.

He was behaving as if she had already gone, ignoring her and making her feel as wretched as she deserved. It was horrible, to be so close to him and yet feel as though he were miles away across the sea.

She went down the stairs shot through with the knowledge of how deeply she had wounded and wronged him. She heard him following. She gathered up her coat and bag from the chair in the hall. Already a sense of desperate loneliness was gathering around her.

'I'll come for my things later,' she said, pulling the door open.

'I'd prefer you to do it when Maisie's at school,' he said.

And that hurt more than anything else.

6

Helen's mother was struggling to be positive and cheery, even though she was still lying flat on her back in her hospital bed. Whenever she tried to sit up she became dizzy and sick. Helen's father sat beside her, his eyes sunk into black hollows of worry.

Helen had brought grapes and magazines and made sure to be careful with her make-up and clothes so as not to alarm her parents with the wild, hunted image she had seen in the mirror when she arrived back at her flat having been so comprehensively dismissed by Ed. Her mind kept reliving the brief and horribly final scene with him.

It was not at all like the severance from Peter. That had been a blow of fate. But this had all been brought about by her own doing.

She ached with shame and loneliness.

And now even her poor parents seemed to have gone beyond helping her, all caught up in their own problems.

★ ★ ★

In the early afternoon she had to leave them both in order to keep an appointment with her new client. Her father walked her to her car.

'We'll get through this, Dad,' she told him, making herself believe it. 'She's comfortable and she's been able to eat a little fruit. She'll get better.'

Her father nodded, looking unconvinced. He looked at Archie, sat quietly on the passenger seat of Helen's car. 'I'll take him home with me,' he said suddenly. 'I hate being in the house on my own. He'll be company for me, make things seem more normal. I'll look after him, don't worry. I'll do it for your mother's sake. I know I've always been hopeless about doing anything except my work. But maybe it's not too late to change.'

'Oh, Dad!' She hugged him, all choked up.

After he had persuaded Archie into his car and she was entirely alone, she rested her head on the steering wheel and wept.

She saw the fat brown packet as soon as she pushed open the door to her flat. The *W1* postmark.

A sickening dread churned in her stomach as she opened it and poured the contents on to her work table.

This time there were around twenty photographs, all with Helen as the central subject, charting her life from around the age of ten to the present.

She was tempted to gather them all up, make a bonfire in the back garden and get rid of them for ever. But if she were to inform the police, she would need evidence. She thrust them into the box in which she kept her fabric scraps, burying them at the very bottom.

★ ★ ★

Eleanor Holt arrived promptly. Today she wore a grey wool coat with a soft pink dress beneath. Her silver hair moved in gleaming waves around her shoulders. She looked carefully through Helen's sketches and the samples of fabric she had obtained for her.

'These are wonderful drawings!' she exclaimed. 'You're very talented, Mrs Lashley.'

Helen managed a faint smile. 'Thank you.'

Eleanor fingered a sample of figured gold brocade. 'I love this cloth.' She looked at Helen and smiled. 'May I call you by your Christian name?'

'Of course.'

Eleanor looked again at the sketches and tapped one with her index finger. 'You know, Helen, I think I'm leaning towards the medieval design made up in the gold brocade. It would look absolutely perfect, exactly what I was hoping for.'

'I could easily make adjustments,' Helen told her, admiring Eleanor's swift decisiveness. 'Either now, or when you have fittings.'

'I rather think we couldn't improve on the perfection of this design,' Eleanor said softly. 'When can we have a first fitting?'

'Maybe this time next week,' Helen suggested, knowing that she would have to work long hours to get to that stage. But then what else did she have to occupy her?

'Splendid.' Eleanor rose to her feet. 'I hope that won't mean you have to work too hard. If you don't mind my saying so, Helen, you look very tired.' Her voice was low and full of sympathy.

'I've a few things on my mind,' Helen said. 'My mother's not well.'

'Oh, your poor mother. I'm sorry to hear that. Is it serious?'

Helen gave a brief outline. She was suddenly totally exhausted and couldn't wait for Eleanor — pleasant as she was — to leave her in peace so she could sit down and lose herself in her thoughts.

At the door, Eleanor took Helen's

hand and pressed it warmly. 'Take care, Helen,' she said.

Helen wandered back into her workroom. The quietness of the flat began to jangle her nerves. She threw on a jacket and went out to a café in Kensington High Street where she ordered coffee and a pastry.

She looked around her at the other tables where families and friends were murmuring over their snacks.

Loneliness pushed inside her like a blade. Ruefully she thought of how much she was missing Archie and considered going to the Battersea Dogs' Home and adopting a large hairy mutt. But in the end she simply returned to her flat.

★   ★   ★

She cut an experimental toile for Eleanor's dress in soft cotton and pinned it around Maud. The sleek flowing fall of the skirt gave her a tiny moment of pleasure. She telephoned

116

one of her fabric suppliers in Soho and ordered several metres of the gold brocade Eleanor had chosen.

The door buzzer sounded. Alarm scraped through her nerves, to be replaced by a blind, panicky hope as she saw Ed standing on the doorstep. The hope was instantly extinguished as she noted the sad pile of her cases around his feet. And a bag containing the partly made *Calamity Jane* costume.

'Will you come in?' she asked hesitantly.

Together they lugged the cases into the hall. In silence. He straightened up after the last one was lined up against the wall.

'Will you stay for a few minutes? I'll make coffee.' She wanted to howl with despair and rage against herself for what she had done to pull herself apart from this lovely man.

He gave her a quizzical look. 'Coffee would be nice.'

He stood in the kitchen watching her

as she filled the kettle and searched for a packet of ground coffee. 'Are you going to be all right, Helen?' he asked.

She turned to face him, her body sagging against the door of the fridge. 'I don't know.'

Sensing her inability to make even the simplest decision, he edged her out of the way and prepared the coffee himself. But her hands were trembling so much she couldn't even hold her mug. She put it down on the counter and left it.

'I'm hurting too,' he said, matter of fact rather than condemnatory.

'Why aren't you at work?' Helen asked.

'The meeting in Brighton yesterday was cancelled. I've nothing urgent to write up. Besides which my concentration is a shade dented.'

She pushed a strand of wayward hair behind her ear. 'If you hadn't come back early yesterday, we'd still have been together,' she said, musing on the caprices of fate.

'Yes — but on a somewhat shaky basis, don't you think?'

She gave a long sigh.

'You had some moments of madness,' he said. 'Or at least that's what I've told myself. But sometimes those moments have a meaning, maybe even a purpose.'

She wished he would stop being so gentle and reasonable. She wished he would show her the anger she deserved, and they could start over again. She simply wanted to be with him, on any basis he would agree to. And it was oh so clear he wasn't going to let that happen.

'And for the record,' he said evenly, 'I'm not having a fling with Liza. She's simply a colleague who is both good at her job and good fun. I'm sorry you had to listen to her breathless message. She talks to everyone like that.'

Helen looked away, her face flushing with humiliation.

He was quiet for a time. 'Have any more photographs arrived?' he asked.

She went into her workroom and dug out the buried snapshots. 'These arrived earlier on,' she said, placing them in front of him.

He sifted through the pictures, his brow creasing in thought. 'Helen, this is not a joke. You must inform the police.'

'I suppose so,' she agreed wearily, sinking into a chair and staring vacantly ahead. 'But I can't see there's any point.'

'I don't think you should stay here on your own,' he said, his voice low and concerned.

'No. And I don't suppose you think I should come back to you and Maisie either?' She looked at him with faint challenge.

'No,' he said quietly.

'Not ever?'

He opened his hands in a gesture of not being able to offer an answer. 'What did you do when Peter died?'

'I went to stay with my parents for a while.'

'Then maybe you should do that

now,' he suggested. 'Parents are very good at tender loving care.'

'Yes,' she agreed sadly. 'But when my mother comes out of hospital she's going to need a lot of help. And Dad seems decidedly shaky.'

'In that case they need you as much as you need them.'

'You're right.' She reached out and picked up a photograph of a teenage Helen. 'Why is someone sending me these pictures from the past?' she wondered, frowning.

Ed considered. 'You are the most likely person to hold the key to that mystery. It's your past in the photographs.'

'And their's too.' She got up and began to gather the mugs and spoons and move them to the sink. 'I'd like you to go now,' she told him, dreading the moment of separation and not wanting to prolong the agony.

He paused beside the front door. They looked at each other. Tears welled up in her eyes. Maybe he'd give her a second chance and put all her cases back in the car and take her home with him, so that she'd have him and Maisie to love once again.

He stepped up to her and touched his lips briefly to her forehead. She wanted to feel resentment towards him for his courteous, detached behaviour which had effectively barred any real discussion of the previous day from the agenda. But all she felt was love and desire.

'I'm here for you if you need me,' he said.

She knew he was referring to her parents' situation and the ongoing problem of the photograph sender. Nothing more.

'Will you tell Maisie I miss her?' Helen said.

'Is that a good idea?'

'Well, just tell her I'll finish the Doris Day outfit as I promised.'

He nodded. 'Fine.'

As he left there was a swelling like a fist in her throat. She telephoned her father and told him she was coming home to stay for a while.

★ ★ ★

The next morning Helen was surprised to see a police car come down the drive of her parents' house. A uniformed officer got out and knocked on the door.

'Are you Mrs Helen Lashley?'

Helen nodded, feeling relief that her father had long ago set off to the hospital to continue his vigil at her mother's bedside and there were just her and Archie in the house. 'Come in,' she said.

The female officer stepped inside. She had a scraped-back pony tail and a solemn expression. 'We've had information that you've been receiving anonymous photographs and notes at your flat in Kensington. Is that correct, madam?'

'Yes. Who's given you this information?' Helen asked.

The officer consulted her notebook. 'Mr Edward Connelly. He telephoned to speak to us earlier this morning.'

'I see.' Helen was not sure whether to be pleased or annoyed at Ed's intercession on her behalf.

The officer recited the brief and accurate details Ed had given and asked to see the photographs and the note which had been left on Helen's car.

'I left them at my flat,' Helen told her. 'They're not the kind of thing you want to carry around. But you're welcome to take them for testing — fingerprints and DNA and so on. Or have I been watching too many TV crime shows?'

'There are a number of tests which could be useful,' the officer said cautiously. 'Have you handled the pictures?'

'Yes. It was hard to avoid it.' She had the impression the officer thought that was a pity.

'Who has knowledge of your address and the make and registration of your car?' the officer asked.

Helen had already been through a possible list on many occasions. 'My parents, one or two friends, a few neighbours. And the people at the garage where I have the car serviced. I can't think why any of them would want to send me pictures of myself. Or how they might have obtained the photographs for that matter. They don't match any of the ones in our family album. I've checked.'

'I see.' The officer scribbled furiously, then looked up. 'Is Mr Connelly a friend of yours, Mrs Lashley?'

'Yes.'

'A close friend?'

'Yes. Well . . . ' She stopped herself, instinctively feeling it would be danger-ous to say more.

'Does he have a key to your flat?'

'Yes. But the photos came through the post, not by hand.' She looked hard at the officer, suddenly catching her train of thought. 'Are you thinking that Ed might have sent these photographs?'

'It's a possibility. A high proportion of personally motivated crimes are carried out by members of the victim's family or by friends,' the officer said formally.

'Yes, I suppose so.'

'Do you suspect Mr Connelly?' the officer asked briskly.

'No. Most definitely not.' Her response was instant and decisive.

The officer threw her a sharp glance. 'Has he handled the photographs?'

'Yes.'

The officer frowned into her notebook. 'And you can think of no-one else who might have a motive? Some grudge against you? An old boyfriend maybe? A disgruntled client?'

Helen hesitated. 'No, I've tried, but I can't. I'm sorry not to be more helpful,' she said, feeling suddenly powerless and heartily sick of the whole business.

The officer closed her notebook and got up. 'I think that's as far as we can go for now,' she said. 'Please let us know immediately if anything further of this nature happens in the future.'

'Don't call us, we'll call you,' Helen murmured as she watched the officer walk briskly to her car.

Quite soon afterwards her father telephoned. 'We've got a diagnosis,' he said, with an air of triumph. 'Viral otitis.'

'What?'

'A virus infection of the inner ear. It's unpleasant but nothing life-threatening. It's been coming on for some time, and it probably explains her two falls. They've given her something for the dizziness and I'm bringing her home.' He sounded as eager and breathless as a young man who has just popped the question and been accepted.

For the first time in the last forty-eight hours Helen's mood lifted a little. 'That's great, Dad.'

'It certainly is. Put some champagne in the fridge. We're celebrating.'

★ ★ ★

'It's so wonderful to be home,' Annette sighed, forking up morsels of the moussaka Helen had prepared. 'And not to feel as if I'm pitching about on a rough sea all the time.' She was still very shaky on her feet, but gradually gaining confidence.

Helen's father hovered around her, his face radiant with relief and happiness. Archie lay across her feet, blissfully contented.

'This is like old times, us all here together eating supper,' her father exclaimed. 'It reminds me of when you were a little girl, Helen. Happy times, mmm?' He raised his glass of champagne, looking first at his wife and then his daughter. 'Cheers!'

Annette raised her glass of mineral water. 'Cheers. And thank you, Helen, for all your help. You've been wonderful!'

Helen felt a tenderness in her throat as she swallowed. She put down her fork.

'There's something I have to tell you both.'

They stared at her in concern.

'I've broken up with Ed.'

'Oh, darling!' Annette reached for her hand.

'I can't bear to tell you the full story now. But . . . it wasn't his fault.'

Her father cleared his throat and threw her a worried glance.

She hurried on. 'And there's something else. I've been on the receiving end of some harassment. Someone's been sending me anonymous mail.'

'Good grief!' exclaimed her father. 'It never rains but it pours. What kind of mail? And what are the police doing about it? I take it you've told them.'

'I don't think there's very much they can do, given they've very little to go on.' She sketched out the details for them, watching their faces grow more and more perturbed.

'It's getting to be a very dangerous and cruel world,' her father observed. 'But I expect that's the standard viewpoint of most staid old codgers over sixty.'

'I'm beginning to feel the same myself,' Helen said. She looked from one of her parents to the other.

'I don't suppose either of you have any ideas on who might have taken photos of me and sent them along for my inspection?'

They both shook their heads.

'No possible skeletons in the family cupboard I should know about?' Helen suggested.

'You're talking about the sort of people I put in my book illustrations,' Annette commented with a little smile. 'But I don't know of any real live ones, not in our family at least.'

★ ★ ★

Later on when Helen went to bed she found it impossible to sleep. She got out the *Calamity Jane* suit and began to stitch a seam. It was always better to sew by hand if you had the time and patience, she thought, gritting her teeth as she drove the needle into the resisting suede. And she wanted this particular piece of work to be perfect.

Whilst she worked her mind threw up a picture of Maisie's shining eager face as she had contemplated the creation of this magical outfit. Tears came to her eyes at the thought she might never see Maisie wearing the costume. Perhaps never see her again.

She woke to a dull headache, overwhelmed with a sense of despondency. This will not do, she told herself. She felt ill with indecision as to whether or not she should simply throw caution to the winds and beg Ed to forgive her. She couldn't reach a conclusion, she couldn't even shape the arguments in her mind.

She showered and dressed and went downstairs to make herself a cup of tea. Her mother was sitting beside the Aga as she walked in, glancing through the morning paper before she began work on her new illustration project.

'Hello, darling,' she said. 'There's fresh tea in the pot.'

Helen poured herself a cup and felt a flicker of comfort as the hot liquid seeped slowly through her body.

'So what's on your programme for today?' her mother asked.

'I'm not sure, Mum.' She took another sip of tea. 'Something proactive, I think. Taking a bull by the horns.'

'Which bull?'

'I've been thinking about my photograph sender.'

Her mother gave a little frown. 'And?'

'Well, for a while I've been persuading myself I haven't any enemies I can think of.'

'But?'

'I've been wondering about Suzanne.'

'Suzanne,' her mother echoed. 'Yes,' she said slowly. 'I can see your train of thought. But why would she want to harass you?'

'She was my friend. And then, suddenly, she was the person I most hated. The woman who betrayed me by stealing my husband's love. And I didn't treat her with kid gloves, you know. I gave some pretty damning interviews to the tabloids on my views of adulteresses — and that one in particular.'

'Yes, I see. But, darling — ' Suddenly she stopped. 'No, I'm not going to caution you. If you want to follow this up, then that's your decision. All I'm concerned about is that you don't put yourself in any danger.'

'Suzanne might have been a strumpet, but I never had her down as dangerous.'

'Maybe those are the ones to be wary of,' her mother observed.

★ ★ ★

Suzanne lived in a dingy flat off the Holloway Road. She had once lived in a beautiful old cottage in Primrose Hill. Her husband had been a composer who wrote theme music for TV costume dramas. When the scandal broke over Suzanne's affairs with Peter, he had given Suzanne her marching orders.

Helen knew little of what had happened to her after that, but she had the address of the flat in one of her old diaries.

It was a Saturday morning and Holloway Road was clogged with cars and vans. Helen sat in an endless queue wondering if she was making a colossal mistake. As she pressed the entry buzzer to the flat she found herself hoping Suzanne was out.

But she wasn't.

'Helen!' she exclaimed, as she opened the door, her face registering shock and then alarm.

Understanding the other woman's unease, Helen smiled reassuringly. 'I'm sorry to turn up out of the blue like this, but I'd like to talk to you.'

Suzanne stared at her helplessly, her face frozen.

'May I come in?' Helen prompted.

Reluctantly Suzanne stepped aside, ushering Helen into a narrow lobby which led into a cramped living room lit by just one small window. Looking around Helen could see that life had not been treating her once-upon-a-time friend all that well.

Suzanne removed a sleeping cat from the sofa. 'Sit down,' she said. 'I'm afraid I can't talk for long. I've got someone coming to see the flat. It's on the market.' She shifted from one foot to the other, looking as though she might turn tail and run away at the slightest hint of any difficulty.

'That's fine.' Helen was wishing most heartily that she hadn't come. She hadn't thought things through, she hadn't planned what to say, how to play things.

Suzanne looked at her curiously.

'I was in the area and I just wondered how you were getting on,' Helen said lamely.

'I'm well. Yes, I'm fine.'

She didn't look it. Her skin was a worrying grey colour and there were dark rings under her eyes. A few years ago she had been a sex-kitten blonde, barely five foot tall, and full of life. Now she looked colourless and ill. All of a sudden, she jumped and ran out of the room.

Helen heard sounds of vomiting coming from the bathroom. She came back into the room and sat down again. 'Sorry,' she said. 'It's nothing serious. Just a bit under the weather.'

There was a silence. Suzanne gave a faint smile. 'That's not quite true. I'm pregnant,' she said.

'Oh! Congratulations.'

'Yes, it's simply fantastic.' Suzanne sat down and began to relax. 'I met this lovely man last year. He's a lot older than me, but he's so generous and so kind. Just what I need. My life's turned around.' Suddenly her face became animated and Helen could once again see the woman who had been her rival for Peter's love.

'I've grown up a lot,' Suzanne said. 'I've stopped being a fool.' For the first time she looked Helen straight in the eye. Her face and her whole manner were saying sorry. 'What about you?'

'I've met a man too,' Helen told her. 'Someone very special.'

'That's great,' Suzanne said. She looked quizzically at her former friend. 'Why have you come? What's the real reason?'

'I'm doing a bit of digging into the past,' Helen said. 'I'm currently on the receiving end of a procession of anonymous photographs. Of me. Both now and in the past. Photos I've never seen before.'

Suzanne stared at her, shocked and disbelieving. 'That's seriously spooky.' She thought for a few moments. She looked up. 'It's not me, Helen,' she said slowly. 'For a start, I don't think I've ever taken any photos of you, let alone mailed them.'

'No, I've just come to the same conclusion,' Helen said. 'You're not a stalking type, in my book. And you're too happy with your own life to want to be meddling with mine.'

They sat in silence for a while. 'Do you think we could be friends again,

Helen?' Suzanne asked.

Helen stood up. 'I don't think so,' she said quietly. 'You remind me too much of a really bad time in my life. Sorry.'

Suzanne made a small wincing sound.

Helen touched her hand as she left. 'But I do wish you all the best for the future.'

7

When Eleanor Holt arrived for her next fitting, she stopped dead in the doorway as she saw her gold brocade wedding gown pinned around Maud. 'Oh, that is simply out of this world. 'Fab', as we used to say in the sixties.' The expression of rapture on her face was like that of a child on Christmas morning.

Helen too was pleased with the way the dress was shaping up. Looking at Eleanor's face as she helped her into the gown she was struck by the older woman's quiet air of radiant happiness. Whilst her face was creased with lines of laughter and sadness she was somehow as beautiful and captivating as any young bride.

'Where are you getting married?' she asked, as she made tiny adjustments to the waistline with a small army of pins.

There was a little pause. 'St Paul's,' Eleanor said.

'Wow!'

'My fiancé has an OBE. So he has the right to be married in the cathedral, you see. He had to write to the Queen to request permission, but that's just a formality.'

My clientele is definitely going upmarket, Helen thought with an inner smile. Automatically she began preparing how later on, over supper, she would tell Ed and Maisie the story of the elderly bride to be married for the very first time in the same church where Prince Charles had married Lady Diana Spencer. And then bleak reality kicked in, hollowing her insides with fresh pain. No more lovely, gossipy suppers. No more . . .

Swiftly she pulled herself together.

When the fitting was completed, she helped Eleanor shrug into her coat, noticing that the label inside proclaimed it a Versace original. 'Goodness me, it's nearly lunchtime,' Eleanor exclaimed glancing at her watch. 'Have I been here so long? The time has simply rushed by.'

'It does that when you've something interesting to focus on,' Helen said, smiling.

Eleanor inclined her head. 'What a wise observation.' She paused for a moment. 'Would you care to have lunch with me, Helen? My treat, naturally.'

Helen's initial surprised reaction was to offer a gracious refusal. But why not, she thought. What else have I to do? And Eleanor seemed a pleasant woman. 'Thank you,' she said simply. 'I'd like that.'

Eleanor telephoned for a cab. 'Where to, duck?' the driver said, as they climbed in.

'Claridges Hotel,' Eleanor announced, turning and giving Helen a little smile. 'It's in Brook Street, West One.'

'I think I'll be able to find it,' the driver jested.

★　★　★

Over a lunch of smoked chicken salad and a bottle of Chablis, Eleanor told Helen a little about herself. She had been born in Cheshire, an only child whose mother died when she was fourteen, leaving her to comfort and care for her grieving father who ran a chemist's shop.

Later she became engaged to a college student she met whilst studying to be a teacher. But her father disapproved and drove him away, as he did with two subsequent boyfriends.

She threw herself into her career, rising to be a head teacher in a primary school and later an education lecturer. Her work was fulfilling and she had many friends. But it was not until she met her fiancé, Oliver, that she had at last found true love. And, of course, now that her father was dead there was none of the old jealousy to contend with.

'That's a sad story,' Helen said with sympathy. 'But you look so happy now. Oliver must be very good for you.'

'He is. He's wonderful. And so loving and generous.' Slipping off the flashing diamond ring on her engagement finger, she handed it to Helen for her inspection.

'It's beautiful,' Helen said. As she handed the ring back she noticed that the ring finger on Eleanor's left hand had a pale sunken band of skin where the ring had sat. Almost as though she wore a broad wedding ring for years.

'By the way, how is your mother?' Eleanor enquired. 'Do forgive me for not asking before.'

'She's getting on very well.' Helen told her.

'I'm very pleased to hear that. You seemed so worried about her. There is nothing like the love between mother and child is there?'

'We are very close,' Helen agreed. She noticed that Eleanor's face had become flushed and bright-eyed as the time had gone on. Probably because she had drunk the lion's share of the wine, as Helen disliked drinking at lunchtime.

'She must be so proud of you,' Eleanor continued. 'To have such a beautiful and talented daughter must be a most wonderful and precious gift for any woman.'

Helen made a non-committal murmur of agreement. She found Eleanor's words and the intensity of her gaze faintly disconcerting.

Getting up she excused herself and went in search of the cloakrooms. Accepting the attendant's offering of a clean white towel and soap she washed her hands and checked her appearance in the mirror.

There's something not quite right about Eleanor, she thought, dampening her hair and patting it into shape. But it was hard to put her finger on just what that something was.

Recalling her father's maxim about never mixing business with pleasure, Helen decided that she must not become any more involved with this client than was already the case.

Walking back to rejoin Eleanor,

Helen was struck once again by the older woman's elegance and the exclusiveness of her clothes. She wondered why someone who could afford Versace was having her wedding gown made by a not-very-well-known couturiere in Kensington.

'Thank you so much for a lovely lunch and for your company,' she told Eleanor. 'I'm afraid I have to get back to my workroom now.'

Eleanor sprang up. 'Of course! I mustn't keep you from your important work. We ladies of leisure forget that others have such busy lives.' She reached forward and kissed Helen on each cheek. 'Take very good care, my dear.'

Walking through the swing exit doors Helen felt a wave of relief as though Eleanor were someone to escape from. Which was clearly ridiculous, but there was a fervour about her that was a touch scary. She hoped Oliver was up to dealing with it.

★ ★ ★

She walked the short distance to Bond Street tube station and travelled back to her flat on the underground, knowing that it would take around half the time the cab would need to thread through the traffic.

Tossing her coat on the hall chair, she pushed up the sleeves of her sweater and went into her workroom. Creative therapy required, she told herself as she picked up the skirt of the gold brocade wedding gown and searched for her needle.

Her eye was caught by a small white vellum envelope, propped against her sewing machine. She saw that her name was written on the front in bold flowing script.

For a moment, on a wing of hope, she thought Ed had let himself into the flat and left her a message. But it was not his handwriting, nor did he use electric blue ink. She noticed the envelope bore Claridges' name and address, and as she tore it open she realised the message must have been

146

left by Eleanor, just before they left for lunch.

Inside there was a photograph of Helen standing at the door of her flat and fitting her key into the lock. She was wearing the clothes she had been wearing the day before. Turning the photograph over she found a short message. *With fondest love, my darling. Eleanor.*

She stood in frozen shock for a few moments. The trill of the phone gave her a start.

'Yes?'

'Don't sound so suspicious, darling. It's only me, your mum.' Annette's voice was more vibrant than it had been for weeks.

'Oh Mum, sorry. Are you OK?'

'I'm doing really well. But what about you? What's the matter?'

'I've had another photograph. And a message.' She paused, swallowing hard. 'It's from one of my clients.'

'Oh, my goodness!'

'I think she must be a little crazy.'

There was a pause. 'Helen, you could be in danger. I'm going to put the phone down right away. You must call the police. Now!'

The line clicked off. Helen reflected for a few moments. And then she called Ed.

He was at the door of her flat in less than fifteen minutes.

She had expected things to be awkward and brittle between them. But he was his usual urbane and practical self. He was her lovely Ed, but the tender kisses and hugs were missing and she could only guess what was going on in his feelings.

Helen was so distressed by her discovery she found it hard to stop shaking. 'I thought it would make things better to put a face to the person who's been taunting me all these weeks. But it isn't. It's just horrible.'

Ed pushed her gently down on to a chair. 'Take some deep breaths.'

'I don't think she meant it,' Helen said eventually. 'I don't think she set out to torment me.'

'Maybe not, but what she's been doing is an act of cruelty and aggression,' Ed said with some heat. 'She's been tampering with your privacy and your past. She's caused you unbelievable tension and anxiety. If she's got an axe to grind with you, or some secret to tell then she should have done it face to face. Not this cowardly sneaking in the shadows.'

'OK. Fair enough.' She slid a quick glance at him. 'Thanks for being on my side.'

He shook his head in despair. 'Oh, Helen, who else's side would I be on? So, what do you want to do next?'

'I'm not sure.'

'I don't think you can just let this go,' he said. 'Her activities could escalate. Or she could target someone else and make their life a misery.'

'Yes, I realise that.' She frowned in concentration. 'What do you think is behind this?'

'Her motive?'

'Mmm.'

He didn't hesitate. 'One of the big three — money, love or revenge.'

'I suppose she must have developed some weird obsession with me. Do you think that's possible?'

'I think she could have been obsessed with you for years. She's certainly got photos going way back into the past.'

Helen closed her eyes. 'Oh, this is awful. And the worst part is she doesn't seem a wicked person. I just can't believe she's put me through such hell.'

'Maybe she's experienced some trauma in her life,' Ed suggested. 'Something which caused real suffering.'

Helen looked up at him. 'Yes,' she said slowly. 'Maybe that's it. In fact she reminds me of how I — ' She broke off, feeling heat rise into her face.

'Reminds you of what, Helen?' Ed asked.

'Of how I felt when Peter died.' She wanted to say so much more, but she was choked up.

'Helen,' Ed said with low intensity, 'between us we will find out what's at the root of this problem with Eleanor and then we'll deal with it.'

'I don't want to go to the police,' she said slowly. 'Not yet. If I can fix up another meeting with her, would you go with me?'

'Of course.'

'The only problem is her answer-phone is always switched off. And I've no address for her, except Claridges. And when I telephoned they told me they'd no record of anyone of that name staying there.'

Ed raised his eyebrows. 'Oh, dear. That is not good.'

'No.'

Ed drummed his fingers on the table. 'Someone must know her. Someone must have an inkling of how disturbed she is. Friends, family.'

'I'll keep trying her mobile.'

'The police could trace the number and find out who the connection is registered to,' Ed pointed out.

'Yes,' She twisted her fingers together. 'I'd still like to give her time to contact me herself and offer some explanation.'

Ed looked sceptical.

'Twenty-four hours,' she said. 'And if she's not in touch by then, we'll go to the police.'

Ed sighed. 'I give in. But promise me you'll drive straight back to your parents when I've left.'

'I promise.' She gathered up her courage. 'How is Maisie?'

He hesitated before answering. 'Sad. She's missing you,' he said, with brutal frankness.

She closed her eyes, recalling their conversation in Prague, when Ed had warned her of the responsibilities of becoming involved in Maisie's happiness, and the power to hurt her. She would never forget.

'Goodbye,' he said gently. 'You know to call me any time.' She looked up and met his glance; long, slow and penetrating. At the door, as he was about to walk away, she stretched up and kissed the side of his mouth. What was there to lose?

That evening, whilst she was cooking supper for her parents, a call came through on her mobile.

The caller introduced himself as Michael Sykes. His tone was calm and friendly. 'Am I speaking to Helen?'

'You are.'

'I believe you know my sister, Jean?'

'No, I'm sorry, I don't know anyone called Jean.'

'Maybe she called herself Eleanor?'

Helen's nerves tingled. 'Yes, I know someone called Eleanor. Eleanor Holt. I'm designing a wedding dress for her.'

There was a pause. 'I see. Well, I think you're talking about my sister.'

'How did you get my number?' Helen asked.

'From her mobile. You've been phoning quite a lot.'

'I needed to get in touch with her.'

'Yes, I can imagine you did.' His voice sounded both ironic and weary. 'And I think I need to speak to you. Rather urgently.'

'What about?'

'I think you can probably guess, but I'd rather not talk over the phone. I live in Surrey, just outside Reigate. Can you get round to see me this evening?'

Helen gripped the phone. Her throat felt tight. 'I'll need to bring someone with me. A friend and advisor.'

There was a sigh. 'I'd rather this was confidential.'

'Mr Sykes, I don't think there would be many women who would respond to an invitation to meet a man they have never met at his house on their own. What do I know of you?'

She suddenly felt very much in charge of herself. She was confident that Ed would support her and determined that she was not going to do anything without his being fully involved. 'My friend knows how to keep his counsel. And he's not from the police.'

A few seconds went by. 'I think we understand each other,' Michael Sykes said. 'I'll see you later.'

It was past nine when they reached Michael Sykes's place. Ed had taken

Maisie to stay with a friend and then driven to Helen's parents' house to pick her up and drive her there. Helen had briefly introduced him to her parents and he had greeted them with his usual warmth and directness. She had felt anxious as she looked on, then absurdly proud. And utterly confused.

The journey to Sykes's Reigate home was only twenty minutes from Helen's parents' house. Helen sat beside Ed, her mind humming with what they were about to discover. She kept glancing at him as he drove. Just being in his presence once again produced tiny surges of happiness.

The house was a converted windmill situated on a quiet minor road linking two villages. Its immobilised sails stood out against the blackness of the winter sky like outstretched arms.

Michael Sykes was waiting at the door. He was a man in his mid-fifties, tall and angular, his silver hair thinning on the crown. His face was deeply lined and his eyes a soft grey.

Helen would have recognised him as Eleanor's brother just by seeing him in the street. She had no need to introduce herself. 'You're Helen,' he said, without hesitation. 'Do come in.'

Helen looked around her seeing white-painted brickwork, beautiful faded Indian rugs, a curling iron balustrade corkscrewing up a spiral staircase. Michael Sykes ushered her and Ed into a semi-circular room furnished with fat cream sofas and warmed by an open log fire.

'I'm sorry to have dragged you out here into the depths of the country,' he said. 'Jean — Eleanor — is upstairs asleep. Her doctor's given her a sedative and I don't want to leave her on her own.'

'Would it be best if I simply tell you what's been happening?' Helen asked, instinctively feeling sympathy for this quietly spoken man.

'I know quite a bit,' Michael said. 'Eleanor arrived here by taxi late this afternoon in a very agitated state. I wouldn't say she was drunk, but she'd obviously had a few too many glasses of wine.

'She was tearful and distressed and kept on saying that she'd made an awful mistake, that she'd 'blown everything'. Eventually I got it out of her that she'd left a message with someone. A message that would make it very clear that she had been harassing that person with unwanted mail.'

'That's quite true,' Helen confirmed. Slowly and gently, she filled him in on the troubling details.

'Oh no!' Michael exclaimed. 'I'd no idea it was as bad as that.' He shook his head in disbelief. 'Although I've known for some time that my sister was in an unusually excitable state. She's been swinging between elation and depression and the psychotropic drugs she regularly takes to control her moods seem to be losing their effect.'

'Is she in psychiatric care?' Ed interposed.

'She's been seeing psychiatrists, counsellors and various therapists for many years. But she's never needed to be hospitalised. Most of the time she behaves like a stable and normal person. Many of her and Oliver's friends would have had no idea that she had psychological problems.

'However, in the past few months she has been particularly edgy and volatile. I knew something was going on, but I had no idea what it was until today. If I had known, I would have taken steps to try to stop it.' Michael Sykes looked steadily at Helen. 'I'm sorry,' he said.

'It wasn't your fault,' she said.

Ed leaned forward towards Michael. 'Could you say something about your sister's possible past links with Helen, and her reasons for sending the photographs?' He was suddenly very much the lawyer, calmly impartial, but determined to get to the heart of the matter.

'I need to tell you something about her life,' Michael said. 'I'll be as brief as possible. I don't know what she's told you, Helen, or which version. But this is the truth as I understand it.'

The story he told corresponded closely with what Eleanor had told Helen earlier, apart from the description of herself as an only child. But there were other significant and disturbing differences.

'My sister was offered a headship in a primary school in Greenwich when she was only twenty-seven,' Michael said. 'It was a big achievement. She needed to move house, but on a temporary basis she stayed at the home of one of her staff colleagues. And in time she fell in love with that person's husband and embarked on an affair with him. The affair has lasted on and off for over twenty years.

'The man concerned rose from being a successful manager in a national manufacturing company to becoming a highly successful venture capitalist encouraging young business talent.

'He's now a multi-millionaire, and he's lavished huge amounts of money on my sister — a house of her own, a luxury car, designer clothes, expensive jewellery. But the one thing he would never give her was his exclusive love and the security of marriage. It's the old story of a man promising to leave his wife, but never doing so. And he's not likely to do it now: his wife would take him to the cleaners for a good deal of what he's accumulated.' He paused. 'And who could blame her?'

'Is this person's name Oliver?' Helen asked. 'Oliver Holt?'

Michael gave an assenting grunt. 'I'm surprised she told you his name. She likes to protect his privacy.'

'She only gave me his Christian name. But she called herself Eleanor Holt. It's not too big a leap to make, is it? And I suppose her using his name shows how desperate she is to be his wife.' With a wedding in St Paul's, and a bridal gown of gold brocade, Helen added to herself.

Michael sighed. 'I was aware that she sometimes used his name, when she was shopping and in hotels and so forth. And for years she's worn a wedding ring, as some kind of comfort for the lack of what she longed for. She really does love this guy, even though he's a liar and a coward who's basically got two women on a string and hasn't the guts to commit himself to the one he really loves.' His tone had become dark and bitter.

'So what is the link with Helen?' Ed asked for the second time. 'And what do you think prompted your sister to start sending photographs?'

'I think the trigger came when Oliver's wife was cured of cancer. She was very ill for some time with a brain tumour, and not expected to live long. And my sister began to hope that at last Oliver would be free to marry her. Then Oliver found his wife a miracle surgeon who performed some daring, innovative surgery. Two years on she's been given the all clear, and Jean has sunk into despair.'

Helen listened in growing dismay to

this tale of betrayal and suffering.

'But what is the link with Helen?' Ed insisted.

Michael got up and poured himself a neat whisky. He raised the bottle in Helen and Ed's direction, but they shook their heads.

'When my sister was thirty she became pregnant. Oliver didn't want her to have it. But on this occasion she refused to give in to him. She had the baby in a private clinic in Harley Street and hoped Oliver would be won over when he saw their child. But he insisted on her choosing between him and the baby. So she put it up for adoption.'

'Oh, no, he must be a monster!' Helen exclaimed.

'If you met him, you'd think him the most charming of men,' Michael said, with savage irony.

'The link with Helen,' Ed persisted.

'Ah yes.' Michael took a long slug of whisky. 'My sister got access to the adoption details. For years she simply kept them as some kind of reassurance that all links between herself and her child were not severed. And then around ten years later, after some terrible bust up when Oliver's wife found out what was going on and the affair broke up for a time, she decided to go and find her baby.' He let his glance rest on Helen's face. 'And that baby was you,' he told her.

8

There was a stunned silence. Ed glanced across at Helen, whose face was frozen in shock.

Ed touched her hand. 'Helen? Can this be true?'

'No! I'm not adopted!' she burst out. This was a shock almost worse than anything she could have imagined.

'Are you sure?' Michael asked, his voice kind but determined. 'Some parents never tell their children.'

Helen felt her stomach twist in panic, as she looked into Michael Sykes's gently enquiring eyes. Jumping up, she rushed from the room and out into the garden where she bent over retching with nausea.

Fumbling in her bag for her phone she punched in her parents' number. Her father answered straight away. 'Are you all right, Helen? How are you getting on?'

'Dad. I just have one question to ask you. And it's not easy.'

'Go ahead.'

'The person we've come to see believes that I'm adopted. That I'm someone else's child. Not yours and mum's.' She held her breath, anticipating a terrible silence while her father processed this bombshell.

Instead he let out a huge guffaw. 'Of course you're ours. I was there when you popped out. It was the most fantastic and frightening experience I've ever had. And there were several other people around to witness it. There is no doubt whatsoever that you're Annette Brown's child. Whether the father is me, well, you'll have to ask your mum!

'But just remember that you've got my nose and you're uncannily like my Aunt Maggie who had a mass of wild black hair.' He sounded so sure and upbeat. She knew that she was hearing the truth. A sigh of relief shook her body.

'Dad, thanks! I'll tell you everything when I get back. I love you both. See you soon. And don't worry about me. I'll be fine.'

Ed was standing beside her. 'I'm getting the idea there's no issue about your parentage,' he observed.

'None whatever, thank God.'

He put an arm around her shoulders. 'You're shivering,' he said.

'It must be the shock of getting some good news for a change,' she said ironically.

'I hope that wasn't a dig at me,' he commented. 'Although I probably deserve it.' he guided her gently back into the house again where Michael Sykes was anxiously awaiting them.

Seeing Helen's calm face he let out a long sigh. 'You're not her child are you?'

'No.'

'So that's just one more of her fantasies which is going to be shattered,' he said wearily. 'I'll suppose I'll have to tell her tomorrow.'

'Would it help for me to speak to her?' Helen asked. 'I'm quite ready to do that.'

'You're a very understanding and sympathetic woman,' Michael said. 'But I think it's probably better if she doesn't see you. Not for a while, anyway, maybe when she's stronger.'

Helen nodded, staying silent in respect of his distress.

'There is something you can do for her,' he said. 'I'd be most grateful if the police were not involved in all this.'

'They are already aware,' Helen told him. 'But they don't know her identity. And I won't be asking them to bring charges.' She spoke with quiet simplicity.

'That is very . . . gracious of you,' Michael said. 'Thank you, Helen.'

★ ★ ★

On the way back to her parents house Ed and Helen travelled in thoughtful silence for a while.

'You were very forgiving,' he said.

'Do you think I was wrong?'

'No, but the lawyer in me was wondering whether to advise a sterner approach.'

'I can understand that. Thanks for letting me do my own thing.'

'That poor woman became fixated on you,' Ed said reflectively. 'You were a beautiful fable to brighten her lonely life.'

Helen was only now beginning to understand the full power of what Eleanor had suffered, and what she, Helen had been for her. And yet she hadn't been her child at all. And even if she had, she would have been nothing more than a sacred, golden image shimmering in Eleanor's distorted fantasies about her lost child.

It was only the parents who had reared you who could fully love your unique individuality, whether there was a blood link or not.

'It's interesting to speculate on how

Eleanor came to believe you were her baby,' Ed said. 'There must have been some mix up in the information she acquired.'

'Maybe we'll never know,' Helen said, so buoyed up by the way things had turned out for her that she felt totally renewed with optimism and self confidence.

She glanced at Ed's profile in the moonlight and her heart contracted. 'There's something I need to tell you,' she said. 'Something I wanted to tell you right from the start.'

There was silence. Helen's heart began to thump. She swallowed and steadied herself.

'It's about Peter. It's something I've only ever talked about to my parents, although at the time he died it was splashed all over the papers and public knowledge.'

She told him the story with calmness and simplicity. How Peter had died whilst on the way to visit his mistress. How the shock had eaten into the roots of her security, and soured her memories of what she believed had been a happy marriage. How she had never been able to talk freely about her pain.

She heard him exhale a long sighing breath. He took one of his hands from the wheel and pressed it over hers. And that simple gesture communicated more than a flood of words of consolation.

* * *

Helen's parents were waiting anxiously for their arrival. Spread out on the kitchen table were drinks and light refreshments, and also the deeds to their house.

'We've been doing some sleuthing,' Helen's father said, rubbing his hands. Since her mother had been recovering from her illness he had become unstoppably happy and almost boyish.

'Darling,' Annette cautioned, 'perhaps Helen and Ed want to tell us what they've discovered before hearing about our investigations.'

'It's a very sad story,' Helen said. 'Let's get on with your sleuthing first.'

Her father ran his finger down a section of the deeds. 'We recalled that the people from whom we bought the house thirty odd years ago were also called Brown like us. It was a bit of a joking point at the time, but, of course, not such a great coincidence, there are a lot of Browns about.'

'And I remembered that they had a baby around the same age as Helen,' Annette said. 'A little girl.'

'So,' Ed said slowly, 'Eleanor, or Jean as she really is, saw the address on the adoption papers, and also the name Brown. Ten years later when she came looking for her baby, and there was this girl living in the house and playing in the garden. A girl the same age, with parents called Brown. Obviously her baby.'

'She took some pictures of me,' Helen said. 'And then over the years she tracked me and compiled an album. How extraordinary.'

'Downright weird, if you ask me,' her father commented. 'Do we really need to hear the gruesome details?'

'Yes, we do,' Helen's mother told him sternly. 'I know you prefer flow charts to tales of human suffering, but you're just going to have to grit your teeth.'

Ed fired the engine of his car and headed back to London. He was feeling unusually humble. Helen's generosity and self-possession in the way she had handled Michael Sykes's revelations had stunned him with admiration. And at the same time aroused a renewed wave of fierce love and desire for her.

But when she had finally brought herself to tell the full story of the events surrounding Peter's death, he had been stabbed with self disgust when he reflected on the way he had so summarily rejected her on that fateful afternoon.

He could forgive himself for being angry, but he found it hard to be easy on himself for the arrogant way he had behaved, taking the high moral ground without any real thought as to what troubles from the past might have been driving her.

Only minutes ago she had offered him a tentative kiss as he left her. He had wanted to sweep her up into his arms and carry her away with him back to his house. But she had turned away, and he could tell that she was drained of all energy, unable to cope with any further emotional turmoil. And maybe he had hurt her so much she could not trust herself to believe in him again.

He knew he was not going to get much sleep that night. There was a good deal of thinking to be done. Strategies to work on. But, after all, he was a lawyer experienced in the analysis of human nature. He could surely find a way to convince her of how much he wanted her back.

Helen slept fitfully, dreaming of Ed and Maisie. But in her dream they were on the other side of a fast-flowing river and there was no way she could get to them.

She got up early the next morning and put the finishing touches on Maisie's Calamity Jane costume. She was pleased with the way it had turned out, and she knew that Maisie would be over the moon when she saw it. That is if she ever got to see it. In a few months she might have grown too big for it, she thought sadly.

She recalled the fleeting sweetness of Ed's kiss as they had parted that night. Throughout the previous evening she had felt they were close again, had even dared to hope for the future.

She had seen them as a real family, how she would be there with Ed as Maisie grew up.

She'd take Maisie to the Battersea Dog's Home to find a pet. She'd be there to support Ed when Maisie started asking tough questions about her birth mother. And maybe, in time there'd be another child to be a sister or a brother for Maisie.

But Ed had said nothing of significance when he parted from her and her flame of optimism had begun to die away. When she looked back on the evening, she saw it as a time of emotional meltdown for all concerned. But now, in the cold grey light of a December morning, she sensed that the renewed heat of the thread of passion between her and Ed was doomed to fade away.

She told herself to stop wallowing in gloom. She would simply take her courage in both hands and telephone him later in the morning. She would simply ask if she could come back with him. Come home to him and Maisie. What could be easier than that? What was there to lose?

Ten o'clock came and went. Ten-thirty and then eleven o'clock. Each time she keyed in his number she instantly cancelled it.

Her heart thundered in her chest, her palms sweated. At eleven-thirty she spoke to herself with great sternness and tried again. Before she could hit the buttons, the phone gave its little trill.

The voice on the connection was a sweet, hesitant treble. 'Helen?'

'Maisie,' she whispered. 'How are you?'

'I'm very well, thank you,' Maisie said in her best polite little-girl tones.

'It's lovely to hear from you.' There was a beating pause.

'Daddy says you've finished the *Calamity Jane* outfit.'

'Yes.'

'He says would you like to come round to our house and bring it? And stay for lunch. And supper too?'

Helen fought to keep her voice from shaking. 'Yes, Maisie. I'd like that very much.'

'And stay forever?'

'Is that what Daddy said?'

'Yes.'

'I'd like that very much too.'

After the connection clicked off, she stood motionless for a few moments, letting the message behind Maisie's words sink in. And then allowing the joy to filter through her system. She made her way downstairs to the kitchen. Her mother looked up from her painting work to wish her good morning. And then she laid down her paint brush.

'Something wonderful has happened,' she said. She stared at Helen for a long moment.

'You're going back to Ed.'

'Yes.'

Her mother stared at her and her eyes grew bright with moisture. 'Ed will be so good for you,' she said softly. 'And you will be a marvellous mother to Maisie.'

'I'll do my best.'

'Now go along and pack,' her mother instructed, 'before I disgrace myself by bursting into tears of happiness for you. It's a real roller coaster, being a mum!'

When Helen arrived at Ed's place there was no parking space in front of the house. She walked down the road, carrying the bag with the precious *Calamity Jane* outfit, packed in layers of tissue. Maisie ran down the steps to the gate, her eyes shining with excitement, as though she couldn't quite believe what was happening.

Helen put down her luggage and opened her arms. Maisie gave a huge grin and started running. Behind her she saw Ed standing at the open doorway. He smiled as Maisie delved into the bag and then hugged Helen tight with joy. He spread his arms in a gesture of welcome. His mouth formed three very important little words.

THE END